SIRANGEL

SIREN MAGIC
BOOK ONE

LUCÍA ASHTA

SIREN MAGIC

Sirangel: Book One

LUCÍA ASHTA

Siren Magic

Sirangel: Book One

Copyright © 2019 by Lucía Ashta

www.LuciaAshta.com

Cover design by Sanja Balan of Sanja's Covers

Editing by Lee Burton

Proofing by Elsa Crites

ISBN 978-1-7986-7094-1

Version 2019.03.09

BOOKS BY LUCÍA ASHTA

For Sonia Isabella,
who makes my life magical

SIREN MAGIC

I STARED AT A SILVER WOLF HEAD, ALL FEROCIOUS teeth and gaping jaws. And it stared back.

Without a doubt, the wolf head was meant to instill fear. I swallowed a sizeable lump of it and wondered if the sea witch would allow me to return home.

Why would anyone place such a frightening knocker on their door? Certainly it didn't bode well that this was where Mulunu had sent me instead of assigning me a comfortable role among our mertribe.

Built in a pocket of forest, the house was larger than the fishing ships that dotted the ocean, standing tall at the end of a very long and narrow dirt drive that had no beginning from where I stood. The house's blue exterior, the color of a deep, stormy sky, was pleasant enough, but the thought of being enclosed by its thick walls made me shiver. My entire life, I'd never been enclosed in anything.

I turned around, hoping to find the way back to

the ocean, when the door was yanked open and the maws of the silver wolf were flung out of sight.

"Well?" the man barked from inside the house. I blinked at him, thinking nothing particularly useful, only that he reminded me of the lifelong sailors I occasionally saw at sea. Scraggly beard, bushy mustache, and a scowl as deep as the crags that edged the ocean. The interior was dark compared to the bright sunshine outside, and the man's blustery eyes were equally dark, like a rolling sea about to fling its sailors to kingdom come.

"If you're waiting for more of an invitation, y'aren't gonna get it," he said.

I blinked at him some more, sure that by then he'd decided I was an idiot. Here was my chance at a fresh start, a place where no one knew me or my history, and I was already blowing it.

"What's it gonna be, lassie?" the man insisted, moving the door back toward me an inch, as if he'd shut the door in my face if I didn't make a move.

"Uh…" I said, just to say something. I wasn't expecting someone like him … so gruff. I wasn't sure what I'd been expecting, since Mulunu hadn't said, but I'd hoped for a more pleasant welcome. "Um, Mulunu sent me." My voice was a weak squeak and I cringed at the sound of it.

The man pulled the door open wider and took a step toward me, narrowing those fierce, tumultuous eyes like he could see through me. "Did she now?"

"Yes, she did." A part of me realized his question hadn't required much of an answer, but this was the part I'd rehearsed since I'd arrived with a thud atop his doorstep in a swirl of Mulunu's magic. "During my coming of age ceremony, her sea crystal told her that I needed to come to land. So she sent me——"

"To me," he said. "As if I have nothing better to do than to babysit wide-eyed lasses who don't know how to handle themselves."

This time when I blinked, I blinked back tears. I was *not* going to let myself cry. If he didn't want me, and my people didn't want me, I'd just find another place to go. I tilted my head high and met the man's piercing gaze.

When he didn't say anything more for a beat, I started to turn, speaking over my shoulder. "I see that you weren't expecting me. I won't bother you any longer. I'll be on my way."

To where? I had no idea. But I still had a certain amount of dignity left, even if I was the only siren in history to be ordered to head to land during her coming of age ceremony.

A callused hand landed on my shoulder and the voice that followed it was gentler than before. "If Mulunu sent you, there must be a good reason. That woman may be wily and old as seashells, but I've never known her to be wrong."

Neither had I, and that's what worried me most.

I turned back to face the man and the open door behind him, peering around his bulky body. He was only as tall as me, but he was stocky and firm all around. He probably weighed twice as much as I, all muscle and gristle. Past him, it was dark as a cavern, with no sunshine or breeze inside. I'd only been on land for a short while and already I missed the ocean as if it were a limb ripped from my body. I didn't want to be here. I hadn't wanted to leave my home. But no merperson of our tribe had ever defied Mulunu, with her gray hair that was so long it pooled around her in the currents like the ink of squid. Her unnerving milky eyes glowed like opals when the sunshine hit them just right.

The man took a step back and to the side, gesturing inside with a sweep of his arm. "Come in, lass. I don't bite."

But he looked like he might, in the right circumstances.

However, Mulunu, no matter how fierce and unyielding in her ways, had never led anyone in our clan wrong. Her magic was the strongest of all my people. *My people.* Yeah, not according to them. I chuckled darkly. I only realized I had when my reaction elicited a curious look from my reluctant host.

"Sorry," I mumbled. "Just thinking about things."

"No crime in that. Better to think than not to, if ya ask me. Come on, in ya go."

Although I stood at the threshold, and "in" was only a few steps away, I steeled myself for the transition. The moment I stepped into this man's house was the moment I accepted my path wasn't aligned with my tribe's. And my clan was all I knew.

The man's eyes softened. My torment must've been apparent on my face.

"Mulunu knows what she's doing," he said. "We're both going to have to trust in that for now."

I nodded, my head feeling as if it were filled with sea sponges, my waist-long violet hair smacking against my back in heavy, wet strands. Before I could talk myself out of it—because I knew myself and I would—I lifted leaden feet, which were as awkward to me as if I were forced to stand on all fours, and walked into the house that looked as worn and hardened as its owner. My bare feet slapped against the hardwood floor, rubbed to a shine by the entrance.

The moment my entire body passed through the threshold, I was zapped by lightning.

I yelped and clutched at my chest and stomach, squirming, trying to get the sensation to stop. Did they have jellyfish on land as they did in water, so transparent that they nearly blended into their surroundings? I didn't see anything like it, but I could barely open my eyes against the pain.

Mulunu had sent me to my death, the sneaky old crone. She hadn't dared to kill me in front of my mother, so she'd sent me away under false pretenses. The reach of her powers obviously extended beyond the ocean since she was the one to deposit me here in a swirl of flashing light and color ... to die.

I hunched into myself, tears stinging my eyes at the pain of it.

"Child, are ya all right?" the man asked, running his hands over my shoulders and back as if checking for injuries.

I jerked my shoulders so his hands would fall away from me, but I could do no more than that to rid myself of the annoyance of his touch. I was dying and I wasn't sure if he was Mulunu's accomplice in my end.

The sting traveled through my body, leaving no bit untouched. I clenched my teeth shut, whimpering, hating that I'd have to share my final moments with a man I didn't know instead of the mother who loved me and would do anything for me—even send me away because she thought it was best for me.

I cried, wishing for my mother so intensely that the feeling only augmented my suffering. She'd lose it when she found out Mulunu had sent me away to die far from her. My mother was kind and gentle, oh, but she could be fierce. She'd tear Mulunu limb from limb, and the crone would deserve it for her treachery.

I collapsed onto the wooden floor, my legs—awkward foreign appendages—unable to hold me any longer.

"Quinn!" the man roared into the depths of the house while continuing to crouch next to me. His voice was loud and ferocious, and I tried to pull away from it. I couldn't take any more stimulation. I was about to lose the fight, I could tell.

Every bit of me had begun to shake so that I could no longer wrap my hands around myself in desperation to claw the pain out. In moments, I more or less collapsed onto the man behind me, who hurried to adjust so he could catch my head before it hit the floor.

"What the hell's going on?" another voice, Quinn's

I presumed, asked. His words were laced with panic. Kind of the second stranger to care that I was dying—unless he just didn't want me to die on the floor of their house.

"I don't know," the Sailor Man said. He bent over my face and pried open my eyelids. I fought him though, my eyes clenched shut against the pain. "It's got to be the ward."

"The ward shouldn't be able to do something like this. It's not set up that way." Quinn knelt by my side, running his hands along the length of my body and then leaning over my face. His breath was warm and just the heat of it made me want to die already. I couldn't take another thing. My body was about to explode.

I opened my mouth to say something, but garbled, slurred sounds were all I managed before giving up.

"Call the witch!" Sailor Man said.

"There isn't time," Quinn said. "We need her to shift or something, to interrupt the magic."

"What makes you think that'll work?"

"I have no idea. But she'll die if we don't try something, right?"

"Yes." Sailor Man's voice was grim. "No body can withstand this for long." He leaned next to my ear, his beard hairs rubbing against my skin and driving me crazy with the additional sensory stimulation. "Shift, lass. Shift. It'll help."

Shift? It was just my luck that I'd be dying and the only useful tips I'd receive would be nonsense. I tried to shake my head, hoping they'd get the drift that I couldn't shift into a damn thing. I'd even lost my siren tail when Mulunu transported me onto land, a few feet away from the spot where I was going to die.

"What's she doing?" Quinn asked.

"She must be having a seizure or something."

Okay. So obviously shaking my head hadn't worked.

"Mulunu is going to kill me," Sailor Man added. "The girl's only just arrived."

"She wouldn't actually kill you, would she?" Quinn asked, though it didn't seem like the time to worry about someone else dying when I was in the throes of it.

"You don't know Mulunu. If this lass is important to her, I'm a walking dead man."

Yeah, well, he was lucky there. I was only important to a total of two people in this world, my mother and my best friend, Liana, and both were oceans away from here.

The pain intensified and I gasped for air. I swallowed big, empty gulps, my eyes popping open like a fish's stuck out of water. That was me, a siren stuck on land, condemned to death for being different. I should've known it would end like this. I was done for before I was even born.

"This is horrible," Quinn said. "She's really going to die." He sounded freaked out. "Why won't she shift?"

"Maybe she can't."

"Then why else would this Mulunu send her to you?"

"Beats me. But the old hag always has her reasons."

I didn't understand much of what they were saying. I mean, I could shift I supposed, kind of. I'd lost my tail when I popped up on the doorstep, and that had never happened before, not once in my eighteen years.

But once I'd shifted into what passed as a human, what else was I supposed to shift into?

My heart squeezed at the pain, my lungs spasmed, and I understood this was truly the end. My eyeballs ached from the strength of whatever was running through me. I closed them for the final time as my limbs seized and trembled violently, making me jump across Sailor Man's lap.

He tried to hold me still by pressing against my shoulders. "Help me," he cried out to Quinn. "Hold her so she doesn't hurt herself."

But that ship had sailed.

I tried to pull in a final breath of peace, figuring this messed up life I'd led owed me at least that. However, I failed even in that. My breath came up short, and I began to choke and cough at the same time, all while my body thrashed around.

Then the shaking subsided suddenly, as if I were already dead.

Quinn cried out. "Oh no, no, no. Come on! This can't be happening."

My sentiments exactly. I was to die without ever seeing the face of the young man who lamented my loss. Figured.

I opened my mouth to pull in air, but felt as if I were drowning, like all the humans who fell into the ocean never to emerge again.

This was it.

Goodbye, Mama. Goodbye, Liana. Maybe my love would reach them wherever they were. Mulunu claimed that I did have magic even if I rarely exhibited it, everything about me so different from the other merpeople of our clan.

Then I accepted my death.

And just as I did, a pop ripped through my dying gasps, so loud it left my ears ringing. I didn't manage to register what was happening before Sailor Man was scrambling out of my way and allowing my head to drop toward the floor.

Thanks for holding me into my death. Immediately afterward, I regretted that my final thought was sarcastic.

You even manage to mess up death, Selene. Way to go.

❧ 2 ❧

A WAVE OF FRESH AIR ENTERED MY LUNGS, SENDING ME gasping for a whole new reason. I swallowed the air greedily, noticing at the same time that my body was no longer in pain. As suddenly as the ward or whatever it was had attacked me, it fled.

The power of a lightning bolt no longer ran through my body, though every bit of it ached from clenching. And the area beside my shoulder blades hurt.

I tried to sit up, failed, but then felt hands on me again. I blinked my eyes open. The man before me wasn't Sailor Man—Quinn, then. But he was blurry, as if I were waking from a deep slumber.

I stared at him, and he stared at me.

Finally, he asked, "Would you like me to help you sit up?" His voice was now gentle, free of his previous panic. His relief was scrawled across his eyes, the ones that caught me and didn't let go, with as many colors flecked through their irises as my favorite seashells on the ocean floor.

I was pretty relieved I hadn't actually died too.

"Do you feel well enough to sit?" he asked again, and I realized I'd allowed an awkward amount of time to pass while I stared at him, his features coming into focus. He was undeniably handsome—for a land person. His short hair was dark and disheveled, framing a pleasant, stubbled face; his lips were bright and plump as they smiled hesitantly at me.

I'd very nearly died moments ago, so I suspected strange behavior, such as gawking, might be expected of me. How fortunate.

I nodded, regretted the movement immediately, but he got the idea and helped push me up to sitting. I couldn't sit on my own, so he leaned against a piece of wall next to the door, and half dragged me, half helped me scoot, so that I leaned against him.

I sank into his firm chest like a boneless sea slug, unable to do much else. My entire body, limbs especially, was as loose as kelp.

He was warm, and the heat of his body helped begin to return the heat to my own form, chilled and missing the constancy of the ocean water. His scent was unfamiliar as I'd never met him before, of course, but it was more than that; he smelled so very unlike anything in the sea. I found that I couldn't identify the scents other than to find them pleasant and crisp. Whatever it was he smelled like, I enjoyed it.

"Is this comfortable?" he asked while he swept hands around my body as if trying to decide whether to offer the comfort of his touch. Finally, he wrapped strong arms around the bare skin of my waist.

"Yes," I murmured, smart enough this time not to move my head to answer. I nestled into the warmth of his embrace.

Sailor Man's face swam into view. "Are y'all right, lass? You gave us a good fright there."

"I-I think I'm all right." But truly, how was I to know? "I'm sore, but okay, I guess, though my shoulders still hurt."

Actually, now that alertness was returning, I realized my shoulders hurt quite a lot. Once more, I tried to reach for my back. My fingers touched something … strange … and I whirled around to get away from it. From Quinn, I presumed.

My vision blurred and my head spun, but I scooted away from Quinn's reach anyway, only to catch this something smack him across the face as he was unable to get out of the way in time.

I went to lean on the door, discovered it still open, and started to fall, until Sailor Man caught me and dragged me awkwardly to lean against the open door.

"You've got to stay still," he said. "Ya'll hurt yourself more or tear your wings."

I blinked stupidly at him, then at Quinn, who stared back at me with concern … but no shock. "Wh-what?" I said.

"Your wings," the gruff man repeated. "You'll tear them if you keep thrashing about like this."

"My what?"

"Do you think she's deaf or something?" Quinn

asked, and I shot him a scowl—or what I thought was a scowl, but could've been anything else in my current state.

"I'm not deaf," I snapped. "I just don't have wings." But of course, even as I said it I knew I must. There was only so far denial could get me. After all, I had touched something soft and fluffy back there.

And it wasn't Quinn, because I was staring straight at him and he looked completely normal for a human, though as beautiful as any of the mermen, and they prided themselves on their stunning looks. An arrogant bunch, they were.

Quinn's face dissolved into confusion, and then understanding, enough to make me wish I had some of that. "She doesn't know," he whispered, more in awe of the fact than their claim that I had wings.

"How do ya not know you have wings, lass?" Sailor Man asked me, his eyes serious, scrunched together as if he were trying to figure out a complicated puzzle. I hoped he was trying to figure me out, because I could use the help.

I opened my mouth to deny the obvious again, but I snapped it shut. Finally, I said, "I've never had wings before."

I wasn't sure I wanted to, but before I could debate, I caught sight of feathery white wings, much like a bird's, and snapped my head front and center, eyes bugging out of my head. "Ho," I breathed, wondering if one could die of shock so soon after nearly dying by ward. "I, ah … I have wings."

Sailor Man and Quinn nodded.

"I have wings," I said again, trying the incredibly ludicrous statement out.

I took another peek, this time at the other wing. Yep, it was there all right, fluffy, white, and long, just like the other one.

I tried moving them. With only a thought directed at them, they opened wide just as I'd pictured them doing, brushing Sailor Man in the face and sweeping across the floor to extend out into the open threshold in the other direction.

"It's incredible," he said, not bothering to move out of the way. "They're so soft." He reached a hand to touch the wing in front of his face and I quickly retracted them.

Obviously my wings were a true part of me. I'd pulled them away without even thinking about it.

I sat there, dumbfounded, though feeling a bit stronger now that lightning wasn't striking me over and over. I scooted another half step back and leaned straighter against the door, the menacing wolf knocker looming above my head.

"So you didn't know you could shift, I take it?" Quinn said, his eyes trailing all across my wings and the rest of me, slowing down as they swept across my curves.

I stared, my brain struggling to register what he was saying, and all that had happened since Mulunu flung me onto land.

"When I asked you to shift, you didn't," he said.

"I didn't realize I could … shift. But … have I shifted?"

Sailor Man chuckled. "I'd say so. What else would you call sprouting wings?"

"Crazy."

He laughed, a deep, booming sound that lit up his eyes, making them seem less stormy than before. "You're right on that one."

But Quinn didn't even crack a smile. "You nearly died. Are you all right? I don't understand what happened. Why did the ward affect her like that? Was it really the shift that kicked her out of its reach?"

Quinn had started talking to me, but he was clearly speaking to Sailor Man now. I obviously had no answers. I wasn't even sure if I was all right.

"The ward shouldn't have affected her like that, that's for damn sure," Sailor Man growled. "It's supposed to only attack those with ill intentions. I doubt this lass would know an ill intention if it slapped her in the face. I'm getting that witch on the phone right now. She'll have to answer to me for this."

I suspected I should have been intimidated by Sailor Man. He'd only grown gruffer since I'd entered his house. His thick sweater was bunched above his elbows revealing swaths of corded muscle winding around his forearms. More importantly, he'd invited me into his home and then his home had tried to kill me.

But after Mulunu, I wasn't as intimidated as I probably should have been. Everything about her was equal parts powerful and creepy. She could sap the life force of any sea creature in seconds, sucking it into the sea crystal that crowned her staff.

"Quinn, you help her to the couch, get her something to drink. Whatever she needs. I'm getting us answers." Sailor Man stalked from the entryway toward the interior of the house.

Quinn nodded and started to rise.

"I don't like having someone in my house I know nothing about, and I like it less when she almost dies," Sailor Man grumbled.

Thanks for the sympathy. "Sorry to be a bother," I said, and belatedly realized I was still too out of it to hide my resentment at finding rejection ... yet again. Hey, on the up side, at least it seemed like my reluctant host hadn't actually set out to kill me on purpose.

Sailor Man stopped as he entered a larger, adjacent space and brought both hands to his hips. He turned to stare at me, but it was as if his attention wasn't actually on me, as if his eyes were someplace far away. He waggled his jaw back and forth a couple of times, then said, "Mulunu is the one that bothered, not you."

I'd expected more from him, this stranger, even though I had no reason to. I was used to tamping down disappointment and I worked quickly to hide it.

As soon as the old man left the room, Quinn was at my side. "Don't worry about him. He grows on you over time."

"How long does that take?"

He laughed, a wonderful sound that sent warmth gushing through my body. "A while. But you'll eventually get used to him."

But would I be around long enough to get used to anyone?

"Can you stand?" Quinn scanned the length of my body, concern etched on his handsome face. Again his gaze lingered as they skimmed my curves. A shiver ran through me that had nothing to do with the chill in the air.

"I think I can stand," I answered, and pulled my feet under me. "But my legs were wobbly to start with."

"Oh? How come?"

"I've never had legs before either."

His eyes widened so that I could make out every multi-colored fleck. I stared as I took in what seemed like every one of my favorite colors of the ocean. "Oh," he said. "You're a..."

"Yes, I'm a siren." I said it like it was both a gift and a curse, because that's exactly what it'd always been to me. "Kind of, I guess," I added, with a glance to my wings. *Wings.*

"We'll get you figured out," he said with confidence I lacked. "Let's start with getting you to the couch."

Unlike Sailor Man, Quinn wore a short-sleeved t-shirt that drew tightly across ample muscles. When he wrapped an arm between my wings and around my waist, his skin seared against my bare flesh, instantly heating me again. Was this normal for the touch of a land person? If so, maybe there'd be good points to being stranded on land.

I let him lead me away, careful of the wings

attached to my back. Though they were large enough to skim my thighs as they hung from my shoulder blades, they were incredibly light. If not for the fact that I was totally weirded out by them, it would have been easy to forget they were there at all.

Liana wasn't going to believe this. Too bad I had no way to communicate with my best friend anymore.

I shrugged away the pang of loss and shuffled to the couch in the strange, dark house that had tried to murder me.

3

QUINN LED ME TO THE COUCH—A LARGE, DARK BLUE overstuffed contraption that looked like it could swallow me whole—but even before I attempted to take a seat on it, I knew it wasn't what I needed.

"What is it?" he asked when I hesitated, running his hand alongside my waist up and down across my skin a few times.

I temporarily forgot what I was supposed to be doing. His fresh scent, whatever it was, filled my nostrils and made me heady. He pressed his fingers more firmly against my flesh as if to prompt me, but it only made my brain freeze for a moment. "Uh, will you take me outdoors instead please? I'm not used to being inside a confined space." The walls and ceiling were pressing in on me. I was finding it difficult to breathe normally.

His face lit up in understanding and he changed directions. "Sure, I wouldn't guess a siren would like to be inside after being used to all that ocean, huh?"

"This is strange for me, that's for sure." The understatement of a lifetime. It was also kind of him to call me a siren and leave out the obvious point that I couldn't be all that much of one while having *wings*.

"There's a spot outside where no one will be able to see us."

"Oh, I hadn't thought of that."

Quinn looked down at me; he was half a head taller than I. "Yes, well, we don't want anyone getting sight of you right now, not until Uncle Irving has a chance to figure out what's going on with you and why this Mulunu woman would send you to him."

"Right," I said, mostly because I didn't know what else to say. The reality was that even Mulunu probably didn't know what to do about me. I'd been an enigma before. Now that wings had popped out of my back, I wasn't sure what to call myself—beyond a freak, a thought that wouldn't do me any good.

Quinn led me toward a sliding glass door and escorted me out of it, his hot hand moving toward the small of my back, searing its outline onto my bare skin. He nudged me onto a shaded patio with an outdoor sofa that had seen better days. Its blue stripes had faded into the tones of an illuminated sky. I shuffled on awkward legs and plopped down as he said, "It's a bit dirty from all the rain and leaves and stuff falling on it. I hope you don't mind."

"I don't care," I said, already missing the heat of his hand on me. "I'm used to all the things in the ocean. This is much better than inside." I finally sucked in a full breath of fresh air, grateful that my lungs were back to behaving normally. I kept forgetting for a few moments that I'd almost died, only to have the realization return all of a sudden, shocking me anew each time.

"Are you cold?" he asked, his gaze blazing a tingling path where it roamed my body. "You're not … wearing very much clothing."

I was wearing more than I did in the water, where merpeople had little use for clothes. This was my first time dressed in anything beyond a tail. "Mulunu dressed me with her magic when she sent me here."

"Hmm, well, apparently she doesn't know how humans dress."

"Oh, is this bad? I'm so sorry." I fidgeted on the outdoor couch. Was he offended because I was wearing too much, too little, or simply not the right clothes entirely?

He smiled tightly. "Trust me, it's definitely not bad. It's the opposite of bad, actually. It's just that a whole lot of your skin is on display."

"That's a problem?"

"Not for me, no. Not at all, not even a little bit."

I relaxed as his smile grew, revealing nice, bright teeth. "You're not what I'm used to," he said.

I offered him a timid smile. I was as out of my element as a tail-less siren with wings could be. "You're not what I'm used to either. All the boys I know have tails." And none of them took so much interest in my body … or in me at all, other than to mock me when they had nothing better to do.

He chuckled. "None of the girls I know have wings."

We shared a few moments of comfortable silence as I took in the lush forest that surrounded us on all sides. Tall trees towered around the house, protecting it as well as the sharp cliffs that sometimes enclosed the ocean. There was green and more rich green as far as the eyes could see. The air smelled pure and reminded me a bit of the scent Quinn put off. "I wouldn't think anyone could see me out here," I said.

Tension replaced the easy space we shared. "Yes, well, it shouldn't be possible. But there are those that go out of their way to make Uncle Irving's business their own. I wouldn't put it past any of them to be spying on the house right now, though there's no real good perch to see this spot since the house shields it along with the trees."

But he suddenly didn't seem all that sure. "Maybe we should go inside though…"

"Do we have to?" I didn't want to admit how much I needed some sense of familiarity. The woods weren't familiar, but they were so much more so than the inside of Sailor Man's—Irving's—house. Trees edged the ocean in places.

"I think we should." His eyes narrowed as they roamed the forest around us.

"I miss the ocean," I blurted out, and then refused to meet his eyes. "I haven't been gone that long and I already miss it."

"I imagine you would. It must be a very different life than the one on land." He scooted a bit closer toward me across the scratchy cushions, nearly pressing his side against mine, stopping just short of doing so. "I'll do my best to help you adjust … assuming you'll stay here." A hopeful tone infused his voice, almost as if he wanted me here with him. My heart pitter-pattered for a few moments, even though he was a land person and probably was only being kind to the strange, awkward girl.

"Do you think I'll be sent somewhere else?" I asked heavily. I'd barely met Quinn, but he was already becoming familiar, someone safe amid a whirling torrent of near-death and wings. I'd rather be in the ocean, of course, but if I had to be here, it would be easier if I could be with him.

"I hope you won't," he said, and my heart gave another little skip.

Silence stretched between us again before Quinn asked, "Your wings, why do you think you have them? I get that you don't know, but do you suspect? Did something with wings, I don't know … bite you or something?"

"Bite me?" I laughed. "Why would something with wings bite me?"

He shrugged, broad shoulders crunching in his t-shirt. "The ability to shift doesn't appear out of nowhere."

"Then why did you tell me to shift when I was dying?"

"Because I figured that's why this Mulunu would send you to Uncle Irving."

I didn't want to seem any denser than I'd already

revealed myself to be, but apparently there was no helping it. "And why is that, exactly?"

"Uh, because Uncle Irving is a shapeshifter. He's an expert in all things shapeshifting. He might not look it, but the man hasn't met a book he didn't want to devour or a source he couldn't ply for information. When Uncle Irving comes asking, people tell him what he wants to know. He can be very … persuasive."

"I must be one of these shifters, then."

He nodded. "But why is the question."

"I'd imagine it's because my father is an angel."

"Your father is an angel?" he nearly yelled.

"Don't announce it to the whole damn neighborhood!" an unknown voice snapped.

Quinn jumped to his feet and crouched as if he were going to attack whoever had entered our space with his bare hands. I went to stand too, but he halted me with a shake of his head, though he didn't bother making sure I understood his message.

No, his eyes were sweeping the back porch and the thick forest that surrounded the house, looking for the intruder. He scanned each uneven paving stone and every shaded corner. He even looked beneath the table next to the outdoor couch; though it was glass, coated in dirt.

I trained my eyes on two … small birds? Or maybe butterflies of some sort? They flew behind Quinn's head.

"Up here, you dingdong," another tiny voice said, and this time I sprang to my feet no matter what Quinn suggested.

Hovering behind him were two flying creatures that, upon closer inspection, I would have said were women if not for the fact they were also the size of hummingbirds, with wings that fluttered equally rapidly, and had ears that culminated in points at the top.

Quinn jumped in front of me, bending his legs and flinging his fists out in front of him, as if he'd protect me with his body.

I chuckled without meaning to. "They're so small. What do you think they'll do to me?"

"Just because something is small doesn't necessarily mean it's inoffensive," Quinn said, eyeing the tiny intruders warily.

"Well, at least the boy has brains. That's something," the tiny woman dressed in crimson said. Her short skirt and top, which revealed her stomach, were similar to my own clothing.

"Stay away," he said.

"Never mind. I take that back," she said.

"We're here to help," said a second tiny woman in sky blue so striking it was nearly fluorescent. "So you can stop preparing for a shift. Trust me, we're harder to catch in your animal form."

"Animal form?" I said, swiveling on Quinn.

"Yeah, I thought that was obvious," he said. "Sorry. I assumed you'd figured that out."

"I hadn't."

"Oh boy," said the diminutive woman decked out in red, from her clothes to her shockingly bright hair.

"It looks like we have our work cut out for us with this one."

"This one? You mean me?" I asked.

"Yep. She's definitely not going to make our job any easier," the blue tiny person said, ignoring me entirely.

"What are you talking about?" I asked.

The second flying woman tsked while shaking her head, tiny strands of red hair sliding across her shoulders. "We're talking about you, obviously, and how hard it's going to be to get you ready."

"Ready for what?" I realized they all thought I sounded like an ignoramus, probably even Quinn, but what did they expect from a girl who'd lived her entire life, up until today, in the ocean?

"Why, ready for the Magical Creatures Academy, of course," the cerulean woman said.

Quinn growled. "Over my dead body."

"That can be arranged, of course," the crimson woman said, and dive-bombed Quinn with a warrior's cry.

I jumped out of the way, uncaring that I looked like a coward in addition to an ignoramus now. That little woman was scary. Her bright red lips peeled back as she laughed wickedly and pushed her hands forward.

"Save yourself!" Quinn yelled to me, as the tiny person dressed in blue joined the other woman in attacking the large, very strong-looking man as if they were his size, though neither of the women was much larger than his pinky finger.

"What the hell is going on out here?" Irving boomed.

The tiny women shifted course mid-flight, turning to face the older man. The one dressed in red tucked her hands behind her back, plastered an innocent expression on her wicked face, and batted her diminutive eyelashes, to great effect. "Oh, nothing's going on. We're just here to collect our recruit."

"You're not taking her anywhere," Irving growled, sounding much like his nephew, only his growl was deeper.

"What's going on?" a voice squeaked from the other side of an apparatus Irving held in his hand. "Irving? Don't you dare ignore me," said the female voice from somewhere inside it.

He brought the thing to his ear and barked, "I'll talk to you later. Just get me my answers."

I couldn't decide who to stare at first: Quinn and the tiny women trying to attack us, or Irving and what must be an even smaller woman inside the small plastic box he held to his head.

"I'll—" But that was all I heard of the woman's tinny voice before Irving pressed a button and tossed the box onto the couch I'd recently vacated.

He stalked the small attacking women. I had no difficulty seeing that he was indeed a predator, and from the way he moved, a very dangerous one.

4

"WHAT THE HELL IS GOING ON?" IRVING ASKED FOR the second time, his narrowed gaze traveling from Quinn to me, and finally to the hovering ladies.

This time everyone but me rushed to answer him. Both tiny women spoke at once, squeaky and hard to hear over the enraged Quinn. "These fairies entered the yard without my permission and attacked us!" he boomed.

Ah, so they were fairies! I'd heard of them, but had never seen one before.

"We did no such thing," one fairy said, flipping her scarlet hair over her shoulder in indignation.

"That's exactly what you did!" Quinn insisted.

She looked at him, deadpan, and said, "All right, maybe we did enter without permission, but we're under the authority of the Magical Creatures Academy."

"Who cares about the Magical Creatures Academy? It has no authority here. You attacked us. You were in the middle of dive-bombing me when Uncle came out. He saw you."

The fairy crossed her arms in front of her chest. "Yes, well, let's not get bogged down in details. Those aren't important now."

"Haven't you heard?" Irving said. "The devil is in the details."

She scoffed. "We're no devils. We're *fairies*."

Irving scowled. "There are times when it's difficult to tell the difference."

The one with azure hair gasped. "How could you say that? Actually, how dare you say that? We're fairies of the highest order. We're special."

"Not in my home y'aren't, especially not when you enter without permission."

"How'd they get through the wards anyhow?" Quinn asked. "What did Naomi say about what happened? Are the wards even working?"

Red Hair chortled. "Oh no, the boy can't even sense when magic's at work." When Quinn and Irving both growled, she quickly added, "The girl here shorted out your wards. That's how we got in."

"It's also what alerted the Academy to her presence here," Blue Hair said. "Whenever there's a surge of unexplained magic anywhere in the world, the school's headmaster finds out about it. So do a bunch of other places—the Magical Arts Academy and all of its other satellite schools, along with the Enforcers of course. Because it was creature magic, we got sent out."

She adjusted her skin-tight blue skirt with a certain amount of pride. "We've been assigned a mission of the utmost importance."

"What did Naomi say?" Quinn asked his uncle, ignoring the fairies.

"She says she doesn't know what happened. She says the ward should have kept out anyone who wasn't invited." Irving and all the rest of them turned to look at me then, and they *really* looked, studying me from top to bottom. "She says she programmed the ward to keep out all members of the supernatural community."

"Ah, well there's your problem now, isn't it?" Red Hair said. "This girl isn't a part of the supernatural community at all yet."

"Hence, our mission," Blue Hair added.

Irving waved his hand as if to actually wave their comments away. The fairies flew another foot away from him as if afraid he might swat them. "I'm not concerned about your mission," he said.

"You should be," Blue Hair said. "We come under the highest authority of the Magical Crea—"

"The Magical Creatures Academy has no authority here."

"Isn't it just a school?" Quinn asked.

Blue Hair gasped so hard she choked and the other fairy had to reach over to pat her on the back between her blur of wings.

"Just a school?" Red Hair said in a murderous tone that had me unconsciously taking a step back— until I remembered she wasn't even three inches tall. I moved forward again with a nervous glance around me, hoping no one had noticed I was afraid of a fairy.

But no one was looking at me anymore. The fairies were glaring at Quinn. Even Blue Hair, who was a bit red in the face from choking, didn't hold back.

"The Magical Creatures Academy is *not* just a school," Red Hair said, spittle actually flying from her mouth in a fine spray. "It's the finest institute of magical learning for any being of the supernatural community, shifters included." She said "shifter" with a certain amount of disdain. "You did register that it's a branch of the Magical Arts Academy, the *oldest* institute of magic in the entire world?"

Quinn shot Irving an unsure glance. The older man laughed a deep bass sound that reminded me of a walrus. Hey, maybe that's what he shifted into!

"Just because something's old doesn't mean it's good," he said, inciting a series of offended gasps and mutterings from the fairies.

"The Magical Creatures Academy, and the *fine* institute it's a branch of, is spectacular not because of its age…" Blue Hair paused to draw in a breath. I hoped she wouldn't choke again; she looked angry enough. "It's the best chance any creature will ever get at a superb supernatural education. You should know when one deals with magic, there's great worth in learning from the trial and error of others."

"I won't debate this last bit. No point in inventing the wheel a hundred times over." But the way Irving smiled suggested that was the only thing he accepted of the fairy's argument.

"Hmph," she huffed, peering at Irving like he was either the stupidest person she'd ever met or the host of a contagious disease—it was hard to tell from her diminutive scrunched-up features.

"No matter where ya want to take her, you're not gonna." The fairies opened their mouths to retort. Irving raised a large hand. "Mulunu sent her to me, which means she's my responsibility, and I'm not sending her anywhere just yet. And I'm especially not sending her to the MCA."

I expected the fairies to argue all over again, but instead they shared worried looks. "You say Mulunu sent her?" Red Hair finally asked.

Ah, so they knew Mulunu. That made sense. Anyone who knew the crone should be frightened of her. Even the greatest warriors of my tribe gave her wide berth.

Irving nodded. "The lass only just arrived. I haven't had the chance to figure anything out yet, especially when Naomi's wards tried to kill her."

"And almost managed it, too," Quinn said, with the appropriate amount of heaviness for my near death.

Blue Hair gulped, her sky blue eyebrows drawing low. "Are you referring to Naomi Nettles by any chance?"

"The one and the same," Irving said. "You know 'er?"

She shook her head quickly, blue hair flying all over the place. "I've only heard of her."

"Everything we've ever heard is bad," Red Hair

added.

"She's a skilled witch, and a skilled witch always has her uses," Irving said.

"Not that witch." The fairy shook her head fervently, crimson hair sliding in a mess across her bare shoulders.

"Even that witch. I know how to handle her."

But Quinn didn't seem so sure from the sudden frown on his face.

Red Hair whistled, and it sounded like a mosquito buzzing near my ear. "You sure know how to surround yourself with dangerous witches, then. Naomi Nettles. Mulunu. You couldn't get much more dangerous than that."

Irving took several steps toward them and the fairies shared a nervous glance. "If you are who I think you are, then you're just as dangerous as they are."

"What? Us?" Red Hair waved tiny hands around, spluttering. "We're harmless."

"Harmless my hairy behind."

I grimaced at the imagery right along with the fairies.

"Now … that was uncalled for," Blue Hair said. "No need to play dirty."

"You were in the middle of attacking me," Quinn pointed out.

"But we didn't attack you, now did we?" Red Hair brought tiny hands to tiny hips while she buzzed in the air around us. "We might have stopped before touching you, you can't be sure. You can't accuse us of something we didn't actually do."

"You were going to do it, for sure."

"No, you're not sure, and that's why I just proved my point."

The fairies plastered triumph on their faces, turning to stare at me again.

"What?" I finally asked. Their small gazes tickled like minnows swimming against my face.

Red Hair narrowed her eyes at me. "Oh, just trying to figure you out."

"By all means, please do."

She laughed, and I really hadn't been expecting that. She said, "I wouldn't trust these buffoons to—"

"Watch who you're calling a buffoon," Quinn growled, but Irving just looked amused.

"I wouldn't trust these *shifters*," she amended, but the way "shifter" rolled across her tongue didn't sound much better, "to figure out anything too important. We'll get you sorted, though. Nessa certainly will."

Irving said, "If the blue one's Nessa—"

"Sapphire," Nessa corrected.

"The blue one's Nessa the Sapphire, which must mean the red one's Fianna the Crimson."

"Which means even an ape like you should be able to figure out that I'm 'crimson,' not red," Fianna snapped.

"So I'm right?" Irving didn't appear perturbed in the least at the insults the fairies hurled as readily as fairy dust, which I was hoping was real. I was in need of all the help I could get.

"You are," Fianna said stiffly. "And if you know who we are, then you know we mean business."

"I have no doubt you do. That doesn't change what I told you. You're not taking the lass anywhere without my say-so."

"Oh, we always get our way."

"There's a first for everything, now isn't there? Even you should know that." Irving actually seemed to be enjoying the banter.

Fianna the Crimson bared her teeth and I jumped a step backward. Quinn moved to my side, draping a protective hand across my shoulders, mindful of the wings that were still there despite my difficulty in accepting them.

His arm felt … nice, and I inched closer to him, plastering my side against him.

"We're under direct orders from Sir Lancelot to bring the girl back," she said.

Irving only laughed some more. "You mean the talking owl?"

"That's precisely who I mean. The headmaster of the Magical Creatures Academy."

"I'm not worried, then."

"You should be," Nessa said, and I wondered at this talking owl. The world on land was already as confusing and overwhelming as I'd feared it would be, and I'd lost my tail no more than an hour ago. The sun was still shining brightly, directly overhead.

I was in the middle of hoping Mulunu might allow me back when Nessa added, "Not a second to lose. Let's get to figuring the girl out."

Answers were the one thing I longed for more than my home.

5

"I'd like answers too," Irving said. "And let's start with what I want since you're on *my* property."

"Property ownership is a ridiculous invention of the modern age," Nessa said.

"You don't seem like you have any problem with property ownership with your constant mention of the Magical Creatures Academy like it's some godsend. Doesn't the Academy own vast property?" Quinn said.

Property ownership did seem like an odd idea when the water and the land belonged to every creature and no creature.

Irving ignored the way Nessa glared at Quinn and barreled on. "How did you know to come find the lass here?"

"Um … my name is Selene," I said. I couldn't take being referred to as "girl" or "lass" one more time.

"Selene what?" Fianna asked.

"Selene of the Kunu Clan." Though I wasn't really, not anymore.

"The Kunu Clan?" Fianna whistled again. "That's a powerful tribe."

"It is." All except for me. I was the anomaly, the sole one who didn't fit in. "My name means 'moon goddess.' My mother named me that because when she gazed upon the moon, she felt close to my father."

"It doesn't matter what your name means," Fianna snapped.

"And why doesn't it?" I tilted my chin upward in defiance, staring hard at the fairy, who hovered at eye level right in front of my face.

"Because we have far more important things to figure out."

That was true, sure, but I'd always found comfort in that one connection to my father, the angel I'd never met and never would.

"Tell us about your father," Fianna said.

"I'll be the one asking the questions here," Irving growled, then pinned me with those eyes that reminded me so much of the stormy ocean. "Tell me about your father."

I shrugged. The wings moved at my back in the strangest of sensations. This would take some getting used to. "I don't really know anything about my father, other than he's an angel, and he and my mother fell in love."

"That doesn't make sense," Nessa piped up. "Angels aren't able to love anyone."

"Well, my father did."

"Whoa." Nessa held her little hands up, a cascade of silver bracelets clinking down both forearms in a rush of musical tinkling. "You don't need to get all defensive here."

I was pretty sure I did. "My father did love my mother. Actually, he still does."

"All right," Nessa said. She was trying to placate me, obviously, but her tone came off as condescending instead.

"They still talk."

"How do they talk?" Irving asked.

I wished I could do more than shrug. "I'm not really sure. My mother says they talk through their hearts."

"Aw, isn't that sweet?" Fianna said, making it sound entirely *un*sweet.

"Actually, it is. My parents love each other."

"I'm sure they do, lass," Irving said. "Your father doesn't come down to see ya or your mother, however, is that right?"

"Not that I know of. My father heard her siren call and fell in love with her beauty from afar. Their hearts merged in a wave of passion, and I was borne from that love."

"Hearts merged, right." Fianna snorted, and I glared at her. She put her hands up in surrender, but didn't retreat from my personal space, continuing to buzz and hover too close to my head. "I'm just saying, supernaturals like to get it on."

I wasn't sure what she was talking about, but I was certain I didn't want to continue in that direction.

"It sounds like a beautiful story," Quinn said as he

stepped closer to me, and I didn't miss that even he implied that it was nothing more than a story.

"It's true," I said, digging my toes into the cold, rough paving stones beneath my bare feet.

"I'm sure it is." He patted my shoulder, working around my wings. I shrugged off his touch, and when he pulled back I immediately wished I hadn't. It was just … why didn't he believe me?

I scowled at every single one of them and pursed my lips shut tight. I wasn't about to tell them anything more if they were going to question every single detail. My mother had told me the story of how my father and she fell in love a thousand times at least. It was the only connection I had to my father.

"The ocean has been known to harbor stranger happenings," Irving said, the only one who looked as if he might believe me. "I've seen things upon the seas that I scarcely believed."

"You?" Quinn asked. "You're the most believing person I've ever met. You even believe in Bigfoot and the Loch Ness Monster."

"Of course I do. If we exist, if they exist"—he pointed at the fairies—"if a half-siren, half-angel exists, why shouldn't they?"

No one replied. It seemed like a pretty strong point to me, especially since it had never occurred to me to disbelieve anything. Life was so much more pleasant believing in its magic. Why would anyone want to doubt it?

Irving stared at me, but this time his attention was softer, friendlier, as if he'd discovered that he and I had something in common, though I couldn't imagine what. After all, he'd just aptly described me as a half-this, half-that freak.

His eyes grew hazy, as if he were far away, before he blinked the memories or longings away, and asked the fairies, "How d'ya know to come here, exactly? The owl told you, but how'd he know she was at this house?"

Nessa gestured toward me with a snap of her head and a bounce of bright blue hair. "We told you. Her magic flared, alerting the Academy. We knew exactly where to find her."

"I have the least magic of all my people," I said, sounding as sad about it as I truly was. That had been almost more difficult than being too different to really belong. Even Liana had more power than I did. *Everyone* had lots more power than I did. Mother especially did. My shoulders drooped beneath my wings and Quinn took a hesitant step back toward me, though he didn't reach out for me.

"Well, you have enough power to set off the Academy's alarm," Fianna said.

"It doesn't seem right that you have alarms about others' magic," Quinn said.

"It is when it's our responsibility to make sure no supernatural poses a risk to themselves or to the community at large. The Enforcers police the supernaturals, but we train and monitor them; that's just as important, if not more. You know the others can't learn of our existence."

"Obviously not."

"Wh-why not?" I asked. "My tribe never hides itself."

"The Kunu Clan makes its home far away from civilization," Irving said, "that's why. You probably rarely see people."

"But when we do, we don't hide."

"But do ya serenade them and change their perception of reality with your song…?"

I didn't answer. How did he know so much about my tribe and our ways? No, not my tribe. It was hard to remember. I had wings. Right. I'd been sent away … to this mess.

Nessa crossed her legs in front of her while she hovered. "Non-magical people aren't equipped to know about us. They'd kill us."

I gasped and brought a hand to my chest. "Surely they wouldn't! What reason would they have to kill us?"

Nessa shook her blue head and actually looked sad. "Such a shame to have to inform someone so naïve of the true nature of humanity."

"That's for sure," Irving said, surprising me. I thought he'd been starting to appreciate me.

The fairies and the shifters shared a moment I didn't fully understand before Irving addressed the winged folk. "So her magic set off some sort of alarm. You received your orders and flew straight here. Ya discovered the wards down due to her magic and proceeded to attack my nephew. Do I have it right?"

"Not precisely," Nessa said, but didn't bother to correct him … because he had it right.

"We didn't 'fly' here," Fianna said.

"Yeah," Nessa said. "We magicked ourselves here."

"That's awesome," Quinn said. "I wish I could magick myself places."

"Don't confuse them for friends, Q," Irving warned. "Fairies are some of the most mischievous and duplicitous of magical creatures."

"I take offense to that," Fianna said, but didn't deny the charges.

Nessa's wings flapped so quickly that I made out no more than a blur of them as she sat in mid-air right in front of my eyes, no more than a foot from my face. At this range, I noticed everything about her. Though tiny, the woman was extremely beautiful, with pleasant features and body. Her mischievous nature was, however, as plain as her bright blue hair. "How long have you had wings?" she asked.

"I got them only when the ward was trying to kill me."

"So your wings appeared when you were near death?"

I nodded.

"Hmm. I'm sure Naomi's ward could have killed you, so it's a good thing."

"Her ward isn't supposed to kill anyone," Irving said. "It's only supposed to incapacitate till I can figure out what to do with the intruder."

"And you trusted her…" Fianna said, as if that were the stupidest move he could have made.

Irving grumbled, but a look of doubt settled across

his face, half hidden by all the bushy hair. He reached for the plastic box on the outdoor couch where he'd tossed it. Would this very small Naomi still be inside it? Or would she have magicked herself away as the fairies apparently could?

"Your wings had never suggested themselves before?" Nessa asked. "You'd never sensed anything there?"

"Nothing. I always looked just like the other sirens," I said. "Even if I didn't feel like one of them." The admission pained me, but the others didn't seem to notice.

"Of course you wouldn't fit in," Fianna said. And Nessa asked, "So you had a tail before, what, just popping up here and sprouting wings?"

"Exactly. Mulunu sent me here, and, well, here I am. No tail." I gestured at my back. "Big wings." In the bright midday sunshine that shone down on us in the open clearing amid so many trees, my wings were a startling white. I caught Quinn staring at them and hoped he wouldn't think me a freak.

"Amazing wings," Nessa said. "I wish mine were like that."

"You're so much smaller than me, the size of a fly," Fianna said. "You can't have wings like that." Nessa was only smaller than Fianna by a smidgen, but Fianna didn't appear bothered by her exaggeration, though Nessa did—plenty; I suspected that had been the point of it. Apparently Fianna liked to annoy. How … odd. Why would anyone choose to be a bother? My whole life all I'd wished for was to make things easy for everyone around me, and I'd been different enough to cause problems no matter what I wanted.

Fianna tilted her red head this way and that, peering at my wings. "The sprouting of wings could have been the burst of magic that called us. The first time any creature shifts, it alerts us."

"It could've also been her own magic fighting the ward," Nessa said.

"True. Either or."

The fairies scanned my body up and down, like I was some kind of odd specimen. Apparently, that didn't cease once I reached land.

"You're saying you have no clear answer?" Irving said, pushing up the sleeves of his thick sweater.

"Not in this regard," Fianna said.

"Then you're of no use to me or her. Get out." And though Irving's beard, mustache, and eyebrows were gray, and his dark hair shot through with silver, his voice contained enough vigor to make the fairies startle.

"Oh, wait. You misunderstand," Fianna rushed to say. "We have plenty of other information you'll want to know."

"Good," he grumbled. "Then let's get inside where it's safer." He scowled at Quinn. "You should've never brought her outside."

"Sorry," Quinn said, and I opened my mouth to claim responsibility for his actions. He shook his head gently, his dark hair shining as it moved beneath the sunlight, and I shut it. Right, we probably didn't need one more thing to distract from the answers I—we —needed.

"Get in," Irving said, and Quinn wrapped an arm around me to lead me inside. His skin was warm, making me realize I was cold. My body was used to being immersed in water. How long would I need to be away from it? When a single shiver ran through me, he pulled me closer, pressing the warmth of his torso against my side. Hmm. That definitely helped.

"And us?" Fianna asked Irving. "You're inviting us inside?"

"For now. Don't get comfortable. I'm liable to kick you out at any moment."

"How wonderful!" Nessa gushed. "He's invited us in."

If the fairies took "for now" as an invitation, then I supposed what I got from the cantankerous old man wasn't too bad.

And at least when I crossed the threshold of the back sliding glass door into the house, dark when compared to the brightness of the outdoors, nothing tried to kill me. That was an improvement. My standards were apparently appallingly low.

6

I claimed the seat on the couch I'd rejected the first time around, but trying to find the way to sit without damaging my wings I fussed like a fish chasing its own tail. I hadn't paid attention at the time, but the outdoor couch had a gap between the bottom cushions and the top ones, wide enough to allow my wings to slip right through.

The couch inside the house was a solid, overstuffed piece of furniture that bulged at the seams. No wing-friendly gaps.

I looked behind me, trying to see my back, when Fianna laughed. "What a pitiful sight. Girl, don't you have the faintest clue how to handle yourself?"

Now, I was usually gentle. Had Liana been here, she would've said I was too timid for my own good, as meek as a minnow. I'd allowed the younger merpeople to torment me largely without comment because I wasn't a fan of confrontation. Today, however, was unlike any ordinary day.

I whirled on Fianna, pinning her and the fairy who flew next to her with livid eyes. The fairies' wings hiccupped and they dropped a couple of inches before righting themselves. Clearly, they hadn't expected my reaction.

"No," I said, my tone more dangerous than it'd ever been. "I don't know how to handle myself. Would you like to know why? Though you didn't bother to ask, you just gave me attitude, because that's all you apparently like to do. I had a tail for eighteen years. Eighteen years! That's a long time to get used to one way of being. Today, I no longer have a tail, I have legs. I've never had legs before. And I have wings. *Wings.* I've never had wings before either. I've never been on land before. So no, I don't know what I'm doing, and I don't think there's a single thing wrong with that. So please excuse me when I tell you to *back off!*"

Fianna and Nessa blinked wide eyes at me as if they were the most innocent of fairies, something I was beginning to suspect might not actually exist. Quinn shifted from foot to foot, waiting to help me settle my wings around the couch. Irving just looked on, expressionless.

The old me would have suffered immediate embarrassment from my outburst. But I didn't figure I was the "old me" anymore. I sure didn't look much like her.

I went back to trying to tuck my wings in some-how, tangling my long violet hair in their feathers and bumping into the dark wood of the tea table that edged the couch while I turned, when one of the fairies hooted.

I snapped my head back around and opened my mouth to let the fairies know exactly what I thought of their mockery, when Fianna spoke first.

"Woo! Finally. It looks like this girl will be interesting after all," she said.

"My name is *Selene*."

"Name's aren't all that important. No need to remind us."

"Actually, names are incredibly important. A creature's name is very valuable when casting magic that relates to them." I nibbled at my lip. I probably shouldn't have told a single person on land my real name. I could've been anyone else. Hell, I would've welcomed the fresh start. Why'd I tell them my name?

"We know all that, silly," Nessa said. "That's why we never tell anyone *our* real names." She smiled self-importantly and I had to resist the urge to swat at the blue-haired little woman—she was buzzing just within reach.

"Still," Fianna added, studying me. "It's good that she knew that. A sign that we'll be able to make something of her yet."

I nearly snarled at the crimson fairy before taking a deep breath. I couldn't let these little women get to me. Sure, they were probably speaking of me as if I weren't there just to bug me. It seemed like the kind of thing they'd do.

As if Quinn was aware of my turmoil, or maybe

they were annoying him too, he reached for my wings. "Here, let me help you."

"Such a gallant boy," Nessa said.

"You should be able to tuck them in or something," he said, fumbling behind me. "Move them together."

I did, but it didn't help.

"All right, let's just have you hang them over the couch. That should work, right?" he asked, but how would I know?

Apparently my face said it all, because he held my wings away from my body while I sat. It hurt when he pulled on them, but only a little, and if I could manage to sit and get all the attention off of me, it'd be worth it.

I landed on the couch with an *oomph*, and my wings didn't tear off. Progress.

"Thanks." I smiled at him, and he returned the smile while he sank into the couch next to me. His eyes sparkled like the inside of an abalone shell. I didn't want to look away.

Irving took the seat on my other side, leaned back, and crossed his arms over his chest, making the muscles in his arms bulge against his sweater. The man was thick and stocky; I suspected he could be as unmoving as one of the trees outside when he wanted to be. His lips disappeared into his bushy beard while he stared at the fairies, who buzzed above the tea table.

"Oh, are you waiting on us?" Fianna asked. The room was sparsely furnished, a couple of armchairs occupying opposite corners of the room from the couch and little else. There was nothing else to distract Irving.

"I am," he said. "You told me you had information I'd want to know."

Nessa giggled a bit maniacally before Fianna flew over and elbowed her. "Of course we do," Fianna said. "But we've had a long journey over here. Surely you could offer us some tea before we get into it?"

I waited for Irving to tell her to take the next current, or whatever the land equivalent might be, out of there. But it was Quinn who said, "I thought you 'magicked' yourselves here?"

Nessa giggled again, unhinged tinkles, before she slapped a hand to her mouth.

Fianna glared at her. "We did, obviously we did, because we said we did. The journey was quite exhausting, however. A cup of tea each would hit the spot and allow us to relax and better remember all we have to tell you."

Fianna and Nessa batted their pretty, tiny eyelashes at Irving, who finally huffed and threw his hands in the air. "Fine. Get them some tea, Q."

Quinn cast the fairies a wary glance before asking me if I'd like some tea as well.

"I've never had any before. Will it cause some strange effect in me?"

Nessa laughed. "No, silly. It's just tea."

"The kind of tea sailors drink when they sing about their loves and losses across the ocean?"

"Definitely not that kind of tea," Fianna said with a wink. "Normal tea."

Whatever "normal tea" was, I waited for it in silence until Quinn returned with a decked-out tray. Irving glanced at the plastic box a few times, waiting on Naomi, I presumed. But she didn't appear to be waiting for him inside it.

Quinn set cups and saucers in front of all of us, including Irving, surprising me by the daintiness of the set. With its delicate china and pretty colored flowers, I would have expected it to belong to a woman.

Quinn poured the fairies two-thirds of a cup of steaming hot water each. "What tea do you want? And do you take milk?"

But he straightened from his crouch when he noticed the fairies undressing. Nessa slipped her skin-tight skirt off and was folding it in a neat pile on the tea table, a tiny bare bottom waving around in the air.

"Wh-what are you doing?" he asked as Fianna tugged her top off and tossed it to the side in a flash of crimson red and fairy breasts.

Irving grunted noisily.

"What? What are they doing?" Quinn asked his uncle, but a tiny splash was all the answer any of us needed.

A second splash followed before Irving said, "Having a laugh at our expense, apparently."

"Not a laugh, a bath," Fianna said happily, sighing in contentment. "It's just what we needed after the arduous journey."

"It couldn't have been that arduous," Quinn

mumbled. "Selene's wings only popped out a few minutes before you arrived."

"Goes to show what you know about fairies," Fianna said. "We don't like to be put out." She closed her eyes and sank into the water all the way up to her neck, the ends of her hair slipping beneath the surface.

"You can say that again," Nessa said with a sigh, smiling so big her eyes were narrow slits. Gentle trails of steam swirled around the fairies as they sank into their teacups.

Quinn stared, and I stared; I really couldn't help it. Irving dropped the plastic box on the table with a plop and took the teapot from Quinn to pour his own tea.

Fianna's eyes opened. "Stop staring, you perv," she told Quinn, who jumped and quickly turned his attention to me. But then his eyes trailed the curves of my body, moving slowly as if he'd forgotten there were others there with us, before he snapped them to the ceiling.

Irving laughed, the sound thunderous. "Ya know that Selene's dressed more than most mermaids?"

Quinn flicked his gaze to his uncle and nodded quickly, his head bouncing, his hair jumping along with it. He received the pot from Irving and hurried to pour me a cup.

"How do you take it?" he asked me, staring resolutely at the cup in front of him.

"I don't know. How should I take it?" I asked. "With cream and sugar?"

Every set of eyes swiveled in my direction.

"I thought you've never had tea before," he said.

"Oh, this girl has secrets," Fianna said. "I like it. Every girl should have secrets."

Nessa nodded fervently. "Absolutely."

"It's not a secret," I said, looking at the fairies. I had no problem with their nudity or anyone else's. In fact, I was finding the top that kept riding up beneath my breasts and the skirt that scratched across my thighs quite cumbersome.

I flicked my long hair over a shoulder, got it tangled with my wings again, and slumped. "My tribe uses magic to view life on land. We get curious. Some more than others."

"But you obviously don't know a lot about life on land," Nessa said, fishing for more explanation.

I shrugged and brought the teacup to my lips. I knew they weren't for bathing, not for someone my size at least. "I never found life on land all that interesting, what with all that goes on in the ocean. I mostly learned from my best friend Liana. She's fascinated by it all and would watch a lot, as often as Mulunu would let her. Mulunu's the only one who can do it. Liana would tell me all sorts of weird things you all do."

Irving's beefy hand jerked out to place his cup back in its saucer, then he turned his entire body to face me. "Could you see the supernatural world?"

"I-I don't know."

"Think, Selene, think." His fierce eyes were back, rolling like a ferocious storm.

"The few times I looked, I never saw anything but people without magic. But I can't be sure no one else saw the supernaturals. Liana at least never mentioned anything. She was always so intrigued by all the gadgets the non-magical people come up with to try to replace magic." I shrugged. "Who knows what Mulunu sees? She's creepy and probably more powerful than every merperson in the entire tribe put together." Including my mom. I fake shivered until it became real, a wave of cold sweeping through me.

Irving pursed his lips and scrunched up his face, his thick mustache and beard meeting. "We need to find out."

"Why?"

"Because the supernatural community is in a frenzy," Fianna said, sounding bored. "It always is."

"Not like this, it isn't," Irving said. "The shifters usually get along better than this."

Nessa sat up in her bath. "Shifters are a fickle bunch who'll fight over anything, anything at all. It's no surprise you're at war with your kind."

I gulped. War? Had Mulunu really sent me into a war? "Does this war concern me?" I asked. Please say no, please.

"Unfortunately, now it does," Irving said.

My heart sank, and Quinn scooted another inch toward me, whether to protect or comfort I couldn't tell, but he was the friendliest of all of them, so I welcomed it. I longed for comfort, for the familiar, no matter how awkward my life back home had been at times.

"And if this lot could feel your magic"—Irving

gestured to the fairies—"we might not have that long before someone else comes looking for you."

"Lots of someones, more like," Fianna said, but the fact didn't seem to bother her.

"Tell me what you know."

"Oh, that?" Fianna said, and Nessa giggled madly again before clamping her little lips shut.

"Yes, *that*. The reason you're sitting inside my home taking a restful bath."

"You'll want us well rested and happy. Because though we don't exactly have information to share—"

"Like you said you did."

Fianna smiled generously. Only Nessa looked nervous. "Exactly," Fianna said. "You definitely want us in your corner. We're good in a fight."

Nessa nodded, eyes sincere. "We're *great* in a fight."

"Now that Selene is our duty, we'll fight with all we have to protect her and get her back to the Academy. And we're an enemy no one ever sees coming." Fianna closed her eyes and leaned her head back against the teacup, arms stretched along its rim, wings hanging over the side.

Soon after, Nessa did the same. The fairies appeared pleased as clams both at their bath and their news—the announcement that I didn't think really counted as news.

I expected Irving to growl something nasty at them, but he didn't. Even Quinn seemed pensive, his fingers playing with the fabric of the couch that separated us. I surely was missing something. After all, I knew absolutely nothing about war. My clan had been at peace since Mulunu ran it. No one dared mess with her, not even the more violent surrounding clans. Our warriors still trained, just in case, but their skills hadn't been called on in centuries.

I looked around, but no one met my unspoken questions. Quinn stared at the wall ahead, where I was certain he couldn't be all that interested in the sole painting that adorned the flat surface, though I loved it. The image was of a stormy ocean, dark and moody and blue. Much like Irving. I was sure he must have picked it out.

"Well…" Irving slapped his hands on his thighs. "I guess we'll take all the allies we can get, even if they're pint-sized."

"Smart man," Fianna said, her red lips extra bright against the white porcelain beneath her. "Now, be a dear and top us off. This hot water is heaven."

I didn't bother to hide my shock as the cantankerous man, lost in thought, reached for the teapot to do her bidding.

He topped off the baths for both fairies before reaching for his own cup and sipping distractedly.

So I sipped mine, enjoying the hint of bergamot in my tea and the way it combined with the cream and sugar. I'd never had something so sweet.

I took in the painting of the ocean across from me, wishing I could dive into those frothing waves. Who knew how long it would be until I could return?

War. What had Mulunu done to me? And more importantly, had she done it on purpose?

7

I'D TRIED TO FIGURE OUT THIS WHOLE WAR SITUATION on my own, but remained at a loss. "I don't understand. Why would the supernatural community care one bit about me? Why would anyone come after me for anything?" No one had mentioned what would happen once these hypothetical pursuers caught up with me, but I had the impression it wouldn't be pleasant.

The fairies, Irving, and Quinn, all turned to look at me at once, and Fianna said, "Don't you get it?" I obviously didn't. "You're special."

"Yeah, I've been told that a fair share of times, but it's never meant anything good." I suspected it didn't now either.

"Oh, special is good," Nessa said. "It's great, actually." She ran a hand through her bathwater, trailing a tinkling sound across its surface.

I longed to be submerged in water too. Since that didn't appear to be an option anytime soon, I trained my gaze on the outdoors—so near and yet beyond my reach. There at least I didn't experience the weight of the walls and the ceiling as if I carried them on my back. The house was large enough to contain several rooms and an upstairs story; every square foot of it seemed to cage me.

"But being special does mean people will try to take your power for themselves," Nessa continued, "or replicate your magic, or try to nullify your magic so your powers can't be used against them." Nessa sounded like she was only just getting started.

"Maybe even kill you," Fianna said, "depending on what you can actually do."

"Kill?" I squeaked.

The fairies didn't have the chance to answer. Quinn's voice was harsh. "Don't either one of you think before you speak? Do you really have to freak her out right now? Can't you tell this has already been a lot for her?"

"No good ever comes from withholding the truth," Fianna said unapologetically, uncaring that they'd bent the truth several times since arriving.

Irving slid to the edge of the couch, his expression grave. "The shifters and vampires who oppose the Enforcers have been more agitated than usual lately. They'll pounce at the chance to turn the tides if they find out about 'er and they think her powers will offer them any kind of advantage. What can you do to prepare her for what's coming?"

"Oh, we each have different specialties," Fianna said, glossing right over the mention of shifters and vampires pouncing that had me swallowing repeatedly. "I'll help her figure out her magic. Mine's the most powerful. And Nessa's a brain when she wants to be. She'll, well..." She peered at Nessa while splashing her toes across the top of her bathwater.

When Fianna deliberated for too long, Nessa glared at her, but I didn't think Fianna noticed. "Nessa can teach Selene to fly."

Nessa looked like she was going to complain for a moment, and then smiled instead. "I can definitely teach the girl to use those splendid wings of hers."

"I suppose that will all be useful," Irving said, drawing the words out and not looking entirely convinced.

Fianna sat up in the bath and turned her entire body to face him, crossing her arms atop the rim of the cup and leaning her chin against them, peering up at our host. Hair clung to her back and shoulders, the wet red so dark it seemed brown. "And what will you be teaching her, old man, huh? How will you prepare her for the creatures that will inevitably come for her?"

"I'll let you get away with calling me 'old man' this once," Irving said, but he didn't sound upset. "Do it again and I'll rip your wings from your back."

The fairies gasped. "You wouldn't," Fianna challenged.

Irving didn't answer, and Fianna squirmed. I guessed he would.

Quinn seemed pleased with his uncle, as if he hadn't liked the fairies pushing him around. I didn't get the impression Irving allowed anyone to push him around often. And he definitely wasn't old—at least he wouldn't be where I came from, where lifetimes usually lasted centuries. He might have been in his mid-fifties, but appeared as strong as Quinn, stronger perhaps because of the power that seemed to simmer within the older man. It was the kind of power that came from experience.

"I'm not sure what I'll end up teaching 'er. I suppose much of it will depend on her," Irving finally said, appearing oblivious to the fairies' scathing looks. Mental note: never threaten the fairies' wings.

"Oh, so you don't know much of anything either," Fianna snapped, but immediately looked like she wished she could take it back. She bit her lip, deliberating. "I mean..."

"Yes, what do you mean, Fianna the Crimson?" Irving pinned his full attention on the fairy, a dangerous energy radiating from his body, though I didn't think he'd actually hurt the fairies ... much.

Fianna gulped and ran her hands through her bathwater nervously. "I mean that ... this is a situation none of us has been in very often, and so it makes sense that none of us would know exactly which is the next best step."

"The best thing to do would be to take her to the Magical Creatures Academy," Nessa said.

Fianna grimaced. "We've already discussed that, Nessa. Irving here doesn't agree on letting her go right now."

"Ever," he interjected.

"Sure," Fianna said, sounding far too compliant. "We can always revisit that later on."

Irving's look said he wouldn't be revisiting it ever, just as he'd said.

I didn't like Fianna behaving so nervously. It didn't suit her; it made me more nervous than I already was.

I couldn't stand the tension. I said the first thing that entered my mind: "What makes anyone think I'll have any sort of powers worth having? I haven't my entire life. Seems unlikely that things would suddenly shift, doesn't it?"

"You've never had wings before either," Quinn said, shooting a meaningful look at where they were hanging awkwardly over the couch.

"Sure, but I had a tail. I've only replaced one for the other." Look at me acting all logical like! That was a good sign. Maybe I wouldn't lose my shells over this after all. "It's not like I've taken on the form of an angel *and* a siren."

Fianna tsked like a know-it-all and I instantly missed her hesitant demeanor. "Just because you don't have both a tail and wings at once doesn't make you any less of a siren-angel."

Nessa nodded her azure head. "What we reveal on the outside is only the tip of the iceberg of what we possess on the inside. No matter what you look like, you're the child of an angel and a siren. As far as I know, there's never been another one of you."

Fianna was nodding. "You can take Nessa's word on that. There's no one brainier in the world of the fae than she." I suspected Fianna was only saying that to placate the smaller fairy. Plenty of stories of the marvels of the fae had reached my clan over the years.

"You're absolutely certain there's never been another siren-angel?" Irving asked.

"In all my studies, I've never run across another," Nessa said.

"And the girl reads more than anyone alive," Fianna added.

"I doubt that," Quinn muttered under his breath. He turned to his uncle. "You've never come across another entry of a siren-angel?"

Irving stroked his beard while he gazed at the same painting of a wild ocean that kept capturing my attention. "Never. I've never even come across the suggestion of the new breed. Angels aren't supposed to come down here to procreate."

"She is a new breed, the first of her kind," Nessa said. Her cobalt eyes widened excitedly. She clapped her hands, her movements making ripples in her bathwater. "That means we get to name her."

"Hey!" I said. "I'm right here and I already have a name, one that I like very much. One that symbolizes my parents' love for each other."

Nessa rolled her eyes. "Not that, silly. The name of your *breed*. You're a new race, see?"

"Maybe I do see, but that doesn't mean I need to be named like I'm some kind of specimen to be labeled. I'm a... I'm Selene, and that's all we need to know for right now." I tilted my chin high, but my bottom lip trembled a bit, overriding the effect I was going for.

Quinn edged closer and I wished he'd touch me. His fingers were outstretched toward me, occupying the space between us on the couch, but his skin didn't meet mine anywhere. I was in the middle of a house, in the center of a bunch of creatures, and I'd never felt more alone.

"You're a *sirangel*!" Nessa gasped, as if I hadn't said anything to the contrary. "Ooh, I like that." The fairy clapped small wet palms together, agitating the water so that it sloshed over the edge onto the saucer. Rays of sun filtered through the sliding glass door to reflect across the water that pooled on the plate.

Fianna surprised me by being the one to say, "Not now. She's had too much for one day. And no one's even tried to kill her yet."

"That witch's ward sure did," I grumbled, rubbing at my chest as if the pain were still present. "Let me get this straight, because I'm still not really under-standing…" Fianna looked at me as if I were about as intelligent as a sea slug, but I powered on. "Why do these other supernaturals want my power so much? Don't they all have their own?"

"Oh dear," Nessa said, and Irving looked at me like I was the elusive uni-horn seahorse.

"Such a shame that this innocence will be lost," Irving said, sounding for the first time like he was ancient and had led a life too filled with loss.

Heat flushed my cheeks. "I can't help being inno-cent if no one will tell me what's going on." Even though they kind of were. "I've been set aside as different my entire life. I've never fit in. I've never been the right anything to be a part of something bigger."

"You misunderstand us," Irving said. "We think it's wonderful."

Fianna didn't do anything to agree, but Nessa nodded her tiny head enthusiastically, and Quinn looked at me with a strange longing I'd never experienced before. His fingers stretched closer, so that I could feel the heat radiating from the tips of his fingers into the flesh of my thigh.

"Innocence in the supernatural world is rarer than a sirangel," Irving said. "To me, it's far more precious."

"Then why won't the supernatural community allow me to keep it, if it's so special?" I said.

"Because the creatures consider our community only in terms of power. In a world where magic abounds, the one with the most of it will rule."

"Only if they wish," Fianna interjected. "The fae hold more power than most, and we don't seek to overpower."

"This is true. If only the shifters and the vampires were like the fae, this world would be far better off," he said. I started at Irving's unexpected agreement. "But there are those among the most powerful who wish to rule the entirety of the magical world."

"That's impossible," Fianna scoffed.

"It is, but they refuse to believe that, to the detriment and harm of everyone else. It is these commanding elements that'll search for you once they learn of ya, Selene. If the MCA knows about ya, it won't be long before the mightiest of the shifters and the vamps come for you."

My chin began to tremble despite my desire to appear strong.

"They won't care that ya haven't explored the extent of your powers," he added. "They'll only care that you're different, a new kind, and so they'll assume that you bring new magic to the proverbial table. They search constantly for that piece that'll allow them to defeat those who resist them. They'll believe you might be that piece."

"But I'm not. I can't be." My voice was little more than a whisper; it was all I had. Power-hungry shifters and vampires? A shiver ran the length of my body, and I sensed Quinn's attention on me. My skin pebbled in goose bumps. It wasn't more clothing that I desired, it was the constant touch of the water. The relative safety I'd found there under the protection of the crazy witch Mulunu.

Irving shrugged, but it wasn't an action of disinterest. "You can't know that ya won't develop strong powers, and neither can any of us. I trust in Mulunu's magic. I've rarely encountered any stronger. Do you trust her magic?"

Reluctantly, I nodded. No matter how much the crone unnerved me, I couldn't deny she was mighty and had never once led our clan wrong. If she'd led me astray, well … I wasn't entirely sure she'd ever considered me a real part of the Kunu Clan.

"If Mulunu sent ya here to me, then there must be a very good reason for it, maybe one even she might not understand. She once told me she doesn't question the magic, she only strives to obey its guidance. She might not even know what part ya have to play on land."

"If she doesn't, how could I possibly know?"

Irving's stormy eyes stared straight into my own. As if I were in the throes of a violent ocean tempest, I met them and held on tightly.

"Ya don't know what you're capable of. You might turn out to be more powerful than Mulunu in the end. But for now, all we need to do is trust in her guidance, in the magic that placed ya here, and work to prepare you so that ya might survive whatever's coming."

The man, who reminded me so much of the sea, clasped one of my hands in his. His callused fingers wrapped my smooth skin like a battered shell that harbored a precious pearl within. "I wish I could tell ya otherwise, but the time for your innocence has passed. You'll have to become a warrior if ya stand a chance at all. We can't guard you at all times, lassie."

I blinked back at him, unable to come up with a single thing to say that would change anything. Yesterday, I'd stood before Mulunu and her glowing crystal with a chance at finding my place among the mertribe. I swallowed hard and blinked some more, sure I looked precisely like the naïve girl he said there was no place for anymore.

He squeezed my hand. "You're a sirangel. I owe Mulunu a debt. I'll see ya through this."

Despite my earlier protests, I'd become a new breed: a sirangel. It seemed it didn't matter at all what

I wanted. How could the course of my powers lie in a path that I'd never have chosen for myself?

My tumultuous thoughts screeched to a halt.

A pop so loud that it left my ears ringing echoed throughout the room, leaving me gaping at what looked like a cloud of fog taking shape before me.

Had the power-hungry supernaturals found me already?

8

IRVING AND QUINN ROCKETED TO THEIR FEET, BOTH OF them moving to stand directly in front of me. White fur rippled along Irving's forearms as he fought to restrain his shift. Quinn growled, setting the hairs across my arms on end; he sounded like an animal, I just couldn't figure out which one.

Even the fairies bolted from their baths, dripping water onto the tea table, unconcerned by their nudity as they squared off to the developing form in the middle of the large room.

"No one's allowed in here like this," Irving growled. "Treat whoever this is as an aggressor."

Red sparks flicked to life in the palms of Fianna's hands, and her hair stood up, electrified by whatever brewed inside her. She pulled back her lips in a snarl, looking vicious despite her diminutive stature.

Nessa uttered words a mile a minute—a spell, I guessed—until finally blue, the same shade as her hair, ignited between her hands. She bounced on the balls of her feet like a fighter—a tiny, wet, naked fighter. Was the fairy, who was even smaller than Fianna, going to physically attack whatever came through?

Just the thought of it made me shoot to my own feet, wincing at the tug at my wings where they met my shoulder blades; I hadn't been careful when I went to stand. I wouldn't let a creature as small as my fingers fight my battles for me, even if I desperately wanted to.

I bounced on the balls of my feet in imitation of Nessa, only much less smoothly since I wasn't accustomed to having feet. I also opened my wings at the ready as she did, but I had no idea what I might do if I attacked. My magic came in the form of influencing others—oh! I tucked my wings against my back, settled on my heels, and waited. All I had to do was sing—unless whatever appeared was immune to my siren song, which had never happened to me before, but my mom had warned me about.

If that happened, I would be back to having no way to protect myself. I searched my mind for answers. What could the other merpeople do, the ones who weren't sirens? What might an angel be able to do? Every thought fizzled before it could take proper shape.

The cloud in the middle of the room began to settle and Fianna shot bursts of red light straight at its center.

"Hold your fire!" erupted a woman's voice from the cloud, along with a flash of green light. "I'm a friendly."

The fairies looked over their shoulders at Irving for confirmation.

"I haven't invited a soul to invade my house," he said, "which means y'aren't a friendly, no matter what you say. Proceed, girls."

Nessa unleashed the blue waves of light she'd amassed between her hands, launched them straight into the center of the fog, which was beginning to resemble a person, and immediately began speaking another spell to reload. She hovered off the table and inched closer to the shape, a woman from the looks of it.

Another eruption of green light flashed, but a second after Nessa's blue hit its intended target, a grunt of pain arrived, and another shout, "It's Naomi Nettles! Cease fire!"

Again, the fairies held their attack positions while looking at Irving.

His thick, bunched shoulders tensed while he wrestled with indecision. "You shouldn't be here, Naomi," he said, but as the cloud dissolved to leave behind a striking, impeccably groomed woman—who was much too large to fit inside a small, plastic box—the ripples of white fur along his arms disappeared and he put up a single hand to indicate that the fairies should wait for his command.

"State your intentions," he barked.

Naomi brushed nonexistent dust from her shoulders, although she'd taken a hit and the gesture seemed pointless. "Is this the kind of welcome you give an old friend?"

"No. You've broken into my house. Are ya here to attack?" White fur began its undulation across his exposed forearms again.

"Of course I'm not here to cause trouble," the witch said in a tone that bespoke trouble. Her head bobbed as she sought me out. Irving and Quinn closed ranks in front of me, doing much to shield me from sight with their bodies, so much larger than my own, but unable to conceal me entirely. I wished I could hide in their back pockets.

"You wouldn't return my calls and I needed answers," she said. "My wards don't fail or attack without reason."

When Fianna's magic made an audible crackle, Naomi spared the fairies her first glance. She smiled at them without feeling, sweeping her calculating gaze up and down their bodies, a frigid gesture that instantly made me dislike the witch, though I hadn't yet decided whether I even liked the fairies.

Naomi arched a perfectly manicured eyebrow at Irving. "Naked fairies? What have I interrupted?"

Irving didn't answer or relax.

"You can stand down," Naomi told the fairies. "Besides, it's not like your magic will harm me."

Fianna stared pointedly at the smoking burns on the witch's forearms, which the sleeves of her form-fitting calf-length dress didn't protect. "We'll stand down when we're certain you aren't a danger, which isn't likely to happen anytime soon. Your reputation precedes you."

"As does yours, Fianna the Crimson, which is why

I can tell you with authority that whatever you throw at me, I'll nullify. You're just wasting your energy with me."

"Well, we're wasting not only our energy, but also our time with you, but for different reasons. Irving?" Fianna said, without taking her attention from the witch. "What's your call? We're ready to take her down."

"Indeed we are," Nessa said from between gritted teeth. She'd completed her spell and held handfuls of bright blue light again.

When Irving didn't answer right away, Naomi took a couple of steps forward in high heels that clicked across the wooden floor, stopped when Fianna hissed at her like a cat, and batted her dark long lashes at the man. "You know me, Irv. I never mean any harm."

"Y'er right. I do know ya. Which is why I know that isn't true. Ya mean harm if it's in your interest to do so. The real question is, what's your interest here and why the hell did you break into my house?"

"Oh, darling," Naomi started, and everyone but me bristled at the endearment. "I didn't *break* into your house. I came here to repair the wards and protect you and whomever you have with you." Again she bobbed her perfectly-coiffed blond head, trying to see around the shifters' broad shoulders, lined up side to side. Quinn reached a hand behind him to pull me closer to him. I pressed against his back, tucking my wings in as tightly as I could in hopes that I wouldn't reveal anything of myself to this witch.

She clicked together nails painted a glossy, bloody

purple. "You hung up on me, remember? So I worried. I figured the best thing I could do would be to show up and help you out, in person."

I didn't believe a word she said; I figured the others didn't either.

"My wards shouldn't have attacked any creature that entered your house at your invitation. I set them up taking into account every known creature. Which can only mean that you must have—"

"Something that's none of your business," Fianna snapped.

"Oh, I think it's very much my business, don't you, Irv?" Naomi batted her eyelashes some more. I wondered how often the move worked that she was so confident that her good looks would be enough to sway a hardened shifter into believing her lies. "All I want is to keep anyone or anything important to you safe from outside harm. My wards are meant to protect, not hurt."

Quinn snorted. "You aren't believing this, right, Uncle?"

Irving hesitated. "What do you really want, Naomi?"

She took another step forward and this time didn't even bother looking at the fairies as they leaned toward her menacingly. "If you have what I think you might have here, then I want to keep it alive."

"Why? What's it to you?"

"Let's just say I don't want certain parties to take control any more than you do. The status quo agrees with me."

"The status quo only agrees with you because you bully everyone else around," Quinn said.

Naomi's eyebrows jumped as if in delighted surprise. "Why, I'm no bully." Her voice dripped feminine seduction, and I responded by pressing even more of my body against Quinn's back. I wanted to yank him away from her—a bit strange given I'd only met him a short while before.

"I just like to get my way. A girl like me deserves to." She batted her eyelashes some more as I peeked around Quinn's shoulder.

"Come out, dear," she said, this time to me. "I won't hurt you. I'll modify the wards so they won't harm you but will keep everyone else out."

"They should've kept you out, that's what they should've done," Fianna said.

"I think I hear a fly buzzing somewhere," Naomi said.

"Fly, my round behind," Fianna snarled and threw red sparks at the witch, whose burns had almost fully healed while she spoke.

A flash of green fog erupted around the witch, intercepted Fianna's attack, and then slid away.

"Watch yourself, *fairy*," Naomi hissed, her eyes still seeking me out. I retreated against Quinn's back again, scrunching my wings in.

"Only if you watch yourself, *witch*," Fianna said. "We know exactly who you are and exactly where you come from. We don't trust you, and we never will."

Naomi whirled on the little red fairy, who continued to defy the witch as if she were dressed in armor instead of fully naked. "Mind your tongue or I'll take it from you." Though I couldn't see Naomi's expression, I had no doubt it was vicious.

"Don't you dare threaten me, you *witch*! Your lineage has nothing on mine. You—"

"Ladies," Irving interrupted. "Table it for now. Naomi, you'll allow Fianna the Crimson to bind your magic—"

"I'll do no such thing," Naomi gasped, turning her fury on Irving, who didn't even flinch.

"Ya will if you want to take a seat in my house and have a cuppa and talk like a reasonable person. Fianna can bind your magic in a way that prevents ya from using it against us only—"

"Fine," Naomi growled, "but I'll be the one crafting the binding."

"All right, but Fianna supervises."

Naomi hesitated.

Irving added, "It's my terms or ya can leave. You're an uninvited guest in my house and I have every right to destroy you for intruding. I'm giving you the courtesy of remaining due to our past dealings, but don't think for a second I don't know what ya're capable of. I won't allow ya to hurt anyone here, no matter what you say or how you pucker your pretty lips."

Naomi tried to look at me again, and Irving said, "Take it or leave it. Ya have thirty seconds."

She took twenty-nine of them before saying, "Fine, but what kind of operation are you running here? The fairies are *naked*."

"Yes, they are." Irving didn't miss a beat. "Q, will you please fetch them some napkins?"

"What about…?" Quinn trailed off.

"Naomi won't hurt Selene, or I'll hurt her."

Quinn nodded, turned to share a concerned look with me, then moved away to fetch napkins for the fairies.

Which meant I was fully exposed to Naomi.

She made the most of the opportunity, smacking purple-painted lips and clicking her polished nails together. The look was unmistakable. She wanted me, and she didn't care what she had to do to secure my power for herself.

I scooted to hide behind Irving's back before he whispered, as softly as he could, "Never hide or show your weakness."

"It's a good lesson," Naomi said. "Strength is a valuable commodity in the supernatural world. You either have it or you fake it."

I was hoping the witch was faking, because if not I worried she might be more powerful than Irving. She looked at me like I was lunch. I didn't move from Irving's side. Her advice might be good, but not when she was the shark and I was the minnow.

❈ 9 ❈

AFTER THE FAIRIES TOWELED OFF, FIANNA RAN A HAND across their small piles of clothing, resting atop the table next to the couch, where Irving, Quinn, and I were once more back to sitting. A flash of scarlet converted short skirts and miniscule tops into what appeared to be battle wear, long pants with thick patches across the knees and long-sleeved shirts of coarse material, which became especially thick across the chest. For the first time in my life, I felt underdressed. Though the fairies' feet remained bare, everything else was covered up to their chins.

I tugged down the top that continually rode up to the underside of my breasts and pulled down my short skirt, but it didn't help much. When I got the chance, maybe I'd ask Fianna to magick my clothes too.

Even Naomi the witch had changed between the standoff and a second round of teatime—one where the fairies actually drank instead of bathed. In a swift burst of green, the witch's lipstick and nail polish color coordinated to a shade of mauve, along with her dress and high-heeled shoes. The burns along her forearms were fully healed, and her appearance was once more impeccable. Regardless, neither the shifters nor the fairies seemed impressed with her. The tension in the air was thick enough to saw through with a butter knife.

Fianna and Nessa sat on the tea table, feet crossed onto their thighs, appearing stranger than usual in their battle gear sipping from a dainty, flowered tea set. "Thank you for the wonderful tea," Nessa said as she tilted a cup toward her lips. "It isn't often that a host is considerate enough to have fairy-sized cups on hand for company."

"Uncle likes to be prepared," Quinn said, as if the fairies were indeed invited company and he and Irving hadn't had a similar conversation with them as they had with the witch.

Nessa sipped contentedly from a cup that was small enough to hold no more than a splash of anything. "Well, it's very nice indeed to enjoy some good Irish tea after all this time."

"You had some just yesterday," Fianna said.

Unfazed, Nessa responded, "Sure, but not like this."

"Do you fairies ever talk about anything that's actually important?" Naomi said in pleasant tones that contradicted the meaning of her words.

"When we're in company we trust, sure we do," Fianna quipped with a tight smile, turning to Irving.

"What's she doing here, really? We can't move forward in suspect company."

I had to agree with the fairy on that front. Time was ticking away, and if shifters or vampires might be after me, I had no desire to waste time.

"Naomi has her uses," Irving said, and I got the impression he was choosing his words carefully despite the aloof look on his face. "If she were to choose to behave, she could be a valuable ally."

Naomi offered a wicked smile as if to say, *Why bother behaving when misbehaving is so much more fun?* Her lips curled in marked mauve lines and she flipped her blond hair across a shoulder with predatory precision.

I scooted closer to Quinn on the overstuffed couch, where I was once more sandwiched between the two large shifters, but I couldn't really get much closer without sitting on his lap. I craved safety, and he seemed to offer his protection without reservation … though it was more than that. There was something alluring about the land boy beyond the security he offered and his warm, handsome looks—though they were undoubtedly part of the appeal. Perhaps it was simply the kindness that radiated from his multi-colored eyes that made me long to be closer to him. But I couldn't exactly throw myself at someone I'd barely met, especially not with all these witnesses.

"And if she were to choose to misbehave," Irving continued, speaking of Naomi though my thoughts had wandered, "then she can be on her way once she repairs the wards."

"So that's it, Irv?" Naomi cooed. "You just want to use me and then throw me out?"

"No one uses you unless you want them to, so I'm not worried." His smile back at her was actually pleasant, as if he were the only one here not terribly bothered by the woman with an obvious agenda. "What do ya say you drain your tea and get to fixing the wards so they're back up and runnin'?"

I stiffened, and Irving sensed it. "Once she crafts the wards in such a way that they account for you, they won't hurt you anymore."

"Of course they won't, dear," Naomi said. "I'll make sure my wards understand you're not a threat. All I need to know is exactly what you are and then I can set about my work." She twirled a strand of her chin-length blond hair and pasted an innocent expression on her face.

I wondered why the woman bothered to speak at all if she was going to do so little to disguise her duplicitous nature. Quinn was already shaking his wavy hair, sending the dark strands bouncing all over the place. "We can't tell her, Uncle. It'll put Selene at too much risk."

"Agreed," Irving said, drawing every set of eyes to him. He adjusted his stocky shoulders. "But it'd be a great help indeed if we could rest safely inside my home while … getting ready."

"Oh, you don't have to be coy with me," Naomi said. "Unless you want to be." She winked lashes coated in deadly black at Irving, who rubbed his beard uncomfortably. "I already know what your plans are because it's the only logical thing, and you, Irv, are a very logical man. You plan to train the girl to defend herself against all those who will come for her, sooner rather than later, I might add."

All those who will come? That sounded like a lot more than a few power-greedy shifters and vamps. I pressed my thigh against Quinn's, wishing his pants didn't impede my skin in touching his. He stared at my legs before resting a whisper of a touch just above my knee. His touch, though light, seared my bare skin, and heat raced across my chilled body—like a gulp of hot tea that warmed me from the inside.

"Yes, well…" Irving said, seeming a bit unsettled. "The sooner we get the wards back to protecting us, the sooner we can focus on other things."

"Precisely." Naomi grinned like a cat with a mouse captured in its jaws. Her mauve lips stretched. I wanted to look away but was bizarrely mesmerized by her face. Here was a witch who'd kill and sleep like a baby afterward, no doubt about it. "And all you need to do for me to fix things is tell me about the girl. I'll even waive my fee."

"You're not waiving your fee, because I've already paid you," Irving said.

"No worries, darling. I don't mind doing you a favor."

"You're *not* doing me a favor, and you won't proceed until you recognize that." Gone was the unsettled Irving. He scooted to the edge of the couch, leaning his elbows against his thighs, and pinned the witch in that stormy gaze of his. She didn't so much as fidget in her place in the armchair across the room, though I'm sure I would have.

"Fine, whatever you say, darling." She waved a manicured hand as if she couldn't care less. But her eyes were ever alert, like a bird's flying across the ocean, seeking easy pickings right beneath the surface of the water. "I always like a satisfied customer. Since I consider you a friend, that goes doubly."

Irving gave a curt nod. I didn't understand exactly what it meant.

"Fianna!" he barked.

"Yes?" Fianna the Crimson replied as if she were docile.

"Will ya supervise Naomi as she binds her magic in such a way that she cannot hurt any of us while in this house?"

"Might I suggest doing away with the 'while in this house' bit? She might have at us the second we step outside of it."

From the gleam in Naomi's light eyes, I was sure that was the case.

"You can't make the terms too broad, *fairy*," Naomi spit out, "or I won't agree to them."

Irving pinned Naomi in a glare that suggested he was ready to back up his threats. "We'll make the terms as we wish or you'll leave. You're the intruder here, and I'm under no obligation to continue extending you any courtesy. Our past dealings have all involved an exchange of payment. I owe ya nothing."

A wave of displeasure raced across Naomi's face before she scrambled to tuck it away. "I'll agree to not hurting any of you so long as, and only if, none of you ever attempt to harm me. If even your intentions toward me harbor ill will, I'll be able to sense it, and the binding will break. I'm warning you."

What exactly she was warning us about I wasn't sure, but I imagined it involved her flashy green magic and a variety of discomfort she could cause with it. I'd seen Mulunu suck the life force right out of sea creatures. In five seconds flat, they went from thriving to dead, and the sea witch had harbored no ill feelings toward those victims. Naomi was ill intentions wrapped in a sophisticated, color-coordinated package. I didn't want to think about what she might do to us if we opposed her.

"Fair enough," Irving said with a nod.

"Great," Fianna said, flying over to Naomi but staying out of swatting reach. "I'm ready when you are."

"Fine," Naomi gritted out. I suspected things weren't going as she wanted them to, even though it seemed as if she'd done nothing but control the situation since she arrived.

With a furious string of staccato words, Naomi ground out, "I, Naomi Nettles of the noble Nettles bloodline—"

"Oh, puh-lease," Fianna said under her breath until Naomi shot her a death glare. Fianna mimed zipping her lips shut and chucking the key over her shoulder. Nessa pretended the key hit her in the head and brought both hands up to her face as she stumbled silently across the tea table, mimicking shrieking cries.

Fianna slapped her on the shoulder. "Hey!" Nessa protested.

"Behave," Fianna said, but her tawny eyes twinkled in amusement.

Naomi cleared her throat angrily. "I, Naomi Nettles of the high and noble Nettles bloodline, do now place a binding on my magic by my own will and according to the following terms: I will not effectuate any kind of harm to any of the creatures seated in this room with me in this moment—"

"No," Fianna said, "that would exclude Nessa and me." Neither of the fairies was sitting. They were standing or hovering in the air above the tea table instead.

Naomi offered a tight smile that revealed that was exactly what she'd been trying to do. "I will not harm any of the creatures currently occupying this space with me *so long as* they have no intention to harm me. If they intend to harm me in any way—"

Fianna interrupted again. "That's too broad. If we have ill thoughts about your sparkling personality, that could be enough to break the binding under these terms. It has to be significant physical harm."

The witch's face tightened all around, revealing her pleasant features as a façade. Her voice became even harsher than before. "I will not harm any of the creatures in this room with me right now as long as they do not intend to do me any significant physical harm. If they should choose to do me harm, the binding on my magic will dissolve, and I shall be allowed to do them harm."

She shot Fianna a snarky look that said, *Satisfied now, you annoying little fairy?*

Fianna gave her a curt nod, red hair shining as the bright midday sunlight from outside glimmered across it.

I liked that there was no end date to the binding. I could do with one less enemy, and Naomi would be a fearsome one.

"I, Naomi Nettles, do complete this binding and seal it with both my magic and a blood offering."

"Blood?" I whispered, gulping.

Quinn whispered back, "The most powerful witches use blood in their magic. The blood of supernatural creatures carries its own magic." He pressed fingertips against my leg in what I assumed was meant as a reassuring gesture, but the firm touch only set my heart to racing.

"Oh, thanks," I breathed, trying to get myself together. Sure, I was a fish out of water, but Quinn shouldn't be getting to me this much...

Naomi traced one of her sharp mauve nails across her wrist and allowed three fat drops of blood to plop to the floor next to her feet, nearly splattering her high heels. Then she waved her other hand across her wrist. A wave of green closed the wound, leaving a faint pink line where her flesh had just been open.

"I bind my magic with my blood," Naomi chanted. "I bind my magic with my blood. I bind my magic with my blood." At the third repetition, the droplets of blood rapidly soaking into the hard wood of the floor ignited into small green fires. In seconds, the green flashes had entirely consumed the blood offering, leaving not even a stain on the floor behind.

Naomi brushed off her hands, though I hadn't seen her dirty them, and cocked a hip to the side, a hand right above it. Several rings on her fingers flashed as the light from outside hit them. "Well? Satisfied now?" she said to Irving first, then Fianna.

The fairy nodded right away and Irving stood from the couch. Immediately, I missed the warmth of having another able-bodied shifter on my other side.

"Thank you for doing that, Naomi," Irving said.

"I wouldn't have done it for anyone else, you can bet on that," she growled.

"I realize that."

"So ... now that we've had tea and you've *bound* my magic"—she said it like one would say, *You've killed my favorite pet*—"are you going to tell me who this girl is so I can get to work or what?"

"Now I'll tell you," Irving said.

"Actually..." I piped up before I could consider the wisdom of engaging the witch directly, "I'll tell you myself."

Irving gave me an approving nod, so I stood as well. Quinn popped up next to me, reaching for my hand. I startled at the unexpected touch and he pulled away his hand, but I reached for it and clasped it in mine.

What had they said? Even if you don't feel strong, pretend that you are? Well, I was about to pretend I wasn't shaking inside and that I accepted the path Mulunu's magic had hurled me upon.

Everyone would see right through me.

❧ 10 ❧

I FORCED MYSELF TO GET THE WORDS OUT BEFORE anyone prompted me; Naomi had already opened her mouth.

"I am the daughter of an angel," I said, unsure why I started with the angel piece when I'd grown up amid a mertribe. Perhaps because the angel bit was obvious, what with the gigantic wings hanging off my back.

I shifted unconsciously as Naomi's gaze raced toward my wings, her eyes wide and stunned.

"Angel wings?" she said, more softly than I thought her capable of. "How … that shouldn't be possible."

All right. So I guess my wings didn't make my heritage obvious. That seemed like an advantage. "What else would my wings be from?"

"Any sort of thing," Naomi said, before Quinn added, "Some of the fae have wings."

"But not like that," Nessa said.

"Some elves do," Quinn said.

"All right, I'll give you that, but it isn't many. Only the special ones."

Quinn nodded, meeting my curious gaze. "There are also some pegasus creatures that have wings."

"I hope I don't look like a horse," I said.

"Oh no," Quinn scrambled. "You don't. You're beautiful, so beautiful. I mean, I'm not saying you look like a beautiful horse. You don't look like a horse at all, you look like a girl. You—"

"Stop while you're not ahead, Q," Irving said, grinning.

Quinn nodded, his cheeks pink even beneath faint stubble. "There are others too. Not who are beautiful, who have wings. Though some of them might be beautiful, I guess. I should just stop, shouldn't I?"

"Definitely," Fianna said, smiling too.

"You could have also been a witch wearing a glamour," Naomi said. "My kind enjoys appearing differently than they truly are. It helps to keep people guessing."

And here I was giving a dangerous witch my secrets. It really didn't seem wise. "Should I continue?" I asked everyone but her.

"Yes, lass," Irving said right away. "We need these wards up immediately, and the only way to keep them from killing ya is to have her exclude your kind."

Fianna added, "I can't do wards like she can." The admission seemed to pain her. "So you'd better get on with it."

I sighed. "I'm the daughter of an angel. I'm also the daughter of a siren."

Naomi gasped. In her surprise, she didn't bother to school her features. For the first time since I'd met her, she appeared vulnerable, like she too experienced the range of emotions the rest of us did. "A merangel?" she whispered, awe dripping from every syllable.

"No," I said. "I'm a siren, not a regular mermaid. My song contains magic, a typical mermaid's doesn't. We're different."

"Oh, I know," she said like a true know-it-all. And suddenly I was back to regretting that I'd had to tell the witch a single thing about myself. I was hand feeding the shark.

"I guess that would explain why you're half naked," she said. "I thought Irving and Quinn were having an orgy when I first showed up. Naked fairies, mostly naked girls."

"What's an orgy?" I asked Quinn with raised eyebrows.

His face colored. "Never mind. It's nothing."

"Oh, it's something all right," Fianna said. "I told you supernaturals liked to get it on."

Oh. I wasn't sure what she meant by "getting it on"—what exactly did what get on?—but I understood enough to keep my mouth shut and not to follow up the point.

Naomi was staring at me. "Amazing… When I set out here I had no idea. I thought it was going to be another one like Quinn, just a little different."

"Like Quinn?" Nessa and I asked in unison.

"Never mind all that now," Irving said hurriedly.

"Naomi, ya need to adjust the wards to include her kind and ya need to do it now."

Naomi, who I didn't imagine took well to orders, nodded her head rapidly. "Yes, you're right. I sense they're closing in."

"Who's closing in?" he asked.

All attention was on Naomi. "I'm not entirely sure," she said. "From the chill of the sensation … perhaps the undead, though the vamps tend to be subtle, unless they're bringing company. But I suppose it could be shifters too, or most other kinds of supernatural creatures, really. The shifters and vamps have been recruiting." She scowled in distaste. "It could be ghouls, the risen dead—the kind necromancers like to mess around with—or maybe ghosts—the kind that have found the way to become corporeal through possession…" She trailed off while she considered, during which time my heart started beating so fast it was in real danger of fleeing my chest, and I reached for Quinn without thinking. He took my hand in his and pulled me against him.

"It doesn't matter much in the end," she finally said. "Whatever's coming, there's more than one, and they're moving fast. And we're definitely not properly prepared for them."

"Then enough with the chatter. Get on with it, woman!" Irving said.

Naomi didn't complain, but snapped to, a sure sign that whatever was nearly upon us was worse than she was.

"I need complete silence and no interruptions,"

she said. "Not even one." She pinned the fairies with warning looks.

"We got it," Fianna said. "Not a peep from us."

Nessa mimed zipping her lips as Fianna had before and went to throw the key over her shoulder, but Naomi cut her with a withering look, so she tucked the imaginary key in the waistband of her skintight battle pants instead. When Naomi turned away, Nessa rolled her eyes theatrically, putting her whole upper body into the gesture, and I bit the inside of my lip so as not to laugh.

Fianna reached over, retrieved the pretend key, and chucked it at the witch's retreating back. The fairies giggled until Naomi spun on one pointy heel to glare at them. Fury lit her eyes from within, and I gulped as I wondered if she might have blasted the fairies right then and there if not for the magical binding Irving made her complete.

Naomi breathed rage through her nose—an act that seemed at odds with her meticulous outfit and grooming—and Nessa giggled, slapping a hand across her mouth, eyes wide.

The witch didn't say another word—and she didn't have to. The fairies behaved after that, though it was possible the whole "imminent attack" thing subdued them as much as the witch's endless supply of death glares.

Naomi plopped into the armchair she'd chosen earlier, crossed one long, elegant leg over the other, and seethed at the fairies. When they only stood upon the tea table looking as innocent as butterflies, she closed her eyes. In under a minute, her breathing grew deep and a slight green glow spread to surround her body.

When she relaxed her face, she almost looked kind. Though if there were a woman far more sensitive than she let on somewhere inside, I doubted she ever let anyone meet her.

She didn't chant a spell like Nessa, nor speak her magic aloud as she had with the binding, but I sensed the energy building around her just the same. For several minutes, there was nothing beyond the subtle glow in her energy field. Soon after that, however, the energy pulsed around her, reaching a couple of feet beyond her, encompassing the chair she sat in almost entirely, top to bottom.

The teacups, abandoned on the tea table while the rest of us stared at her, rattled in their delicate saucers. Next, the glass in the sliding back door shook. The teapot on the stovetop began to whistle, though no flame burned beneath it.

Tension built, straining against me. I longed to pull away from it and hide, but there was nowhere to go, really, not if I wasn't allowed outside. And I especially wasn't going to defy Irving on that if creatures were hunting me. Besides, I didn't want to miss a moment of the witch's unfurled powers. I'd always been curious about magic, probably because I had so little of it myself. And underwater, the magic was different from this. There, power undulated in waves like water currents, or it bubbled and drifted. Sometimes, if it was powerful enough, it whisked outward like a shock-wave. There was none of this glow of light, not even from the large sea crystal Mulunu wielded atop her staff.

I swallowed, and the breath lodged in my throat. My chest felt as if something heavy lay upon it. My hands tingled as if I were meant to do something right then, though I couldn't imagine what.

The prickling sensation raced across all parts of my body, sweeping down my legs and tingling through my toes. I clenched them against the wood floor. What was going on? No one else seemed to be reacting to Naomi's magic like this. They appeared as mesmerized as I was, but that was the extent of it.

When the tingling expanded to reach my wings, it became painful and I took several hurried steps back from Naomi. I gasped as sudden agony raced through my body, boiling my blood. I retreated, stumbling, until my wings pressed against the glass of the sliding-glass door. The vibration of the glass made me jump as if it were on fire.

I was sure I looked like a cornered fish when Quinn sought me out, the only one to look for me when the real show was seated in the armchair. His eyebrows shot up and he moved toward me, drawing everyone's attention, save Naomi's.

The feathers began to rise from their natural position flush against the shell of my wings, and for a few moments I felt as if my tail were back where it belonged. The stinging rush of what?—magic? power? desperation?—created phantom sensations across my legs.

"Selene," Quinn whispered, so softly that I wasn't sure he'd actually spoken. "Are you all right?" He placed a hand against my upper arm and I jumped and recoiled at the way his skin seared my flesh. He yanked his hand back, but it wasn't him, it was whatever was happening to me. Any touch would have been too much with the amount of energy that coursed through me.

"What's wrong?" he asked, his voice insistent, his eyes sharp as they scanned the entirety of my form searching for the cause of my pain.

I didn't respond, because I didn't know what to say, since I didn't know what was wrong. Forming words would have required more focus than I had anyway. Apparently, my non-response was all the response he needed.

He didn't even ask before he wrapped strong arms around me, persisting even when I winced, encircling me in his tight embrace. I trembled as his warmth sent a new wave of fire burning through me. Everything about me was on fire as if with the sting of a thousand medusa jellyfish.

But he only drew me in closer.

My breath came too fast, my heart like a frantic drum … until I allowed myself to feel beyond myself and into him.

The moment I sensed his strength, my entire body relaxed and the pain drifted away. I was able to breathe again. The tension fled my body as I listened to his thundering heart. I breathed in his crisp scent, a bit like the woods outside, and thought of nothing else until a burst of green light slammed into us both.

It clawed and tore at me, threatening to rip me apart.

I clutched at Quinn's ribcage and gritted my teeth, wondering if I was the only one shaking or if Quinn was shaking too. It was impossible to tell.

I clenched my eyes shut and hoped I'd survive.

🎇 I I 🎇

A LOUD BUZZING ERUPTED IN MY HEAD, DISORIENTING me further. As if Quinn sensed that, he pressed me more tightly against his body, and just in time too. My legs gave out in a drastic wobble that would've otherwise sent me crashing to the floor. His hands latched firmly in a loop around my lower back, working around the wings that stretched toward the floor as I slumped.

When the buzzing began to subside, the first thing I heard was an enraged Fianna: "You!" she was saying. "You did something to her. What'd you do? You take it back right now or I'll have at you!"

"I didn't do anything to her," Naomi answered, her voice equally menacing, seething with dangerous tones. "I couldn't have, or has your addled brain already forgotten the oath you made me swear to? You can have at me all you want, because that will be enough to break the binding, and I can't wait to have my magic wrap around your delicate little throat and throttle the life out of you!"

I forced my eyes open to view the room through tunnel vision, the edges blurred and dark, but everything looked the same as it had before. The pain was now absent, but I couldn't yet hold myself up on legs that hadn't worked well to begin with. I slumped into Quinn, who didn't protest at propping me up. He stared down at me, and when I met his gaze I found more worry than seemed reasonable for a man who'd only just met me.

Magic crackled in the room. I dragged my gaze to the others with reluctance. Quinn made me feel safe. The fairies and witch … not so much.

Fianna and Nessa's wings buzzed a league a minute as the fairies drew side by side in the open center of the room. Power flowed between each of their hands, though I hadn't registered Nessa chanting a spell.

Naomi bolted from the armchair and stalked closer to the fairies, her heels sounding out an ominous click clack across the floor. Green sparked to life between her hands too. "Go ahead, *fairies*. I can't wait."

"Enough!" Irving roared, and he sounded like a lion, but hoarser. "You lasses had better get it together, and fast, or I'm booting ya out of my house without a second thought."

Crimson, sapphire, and green magic continued to crackle, no one backing down. Fianna zipped another foot closer, tawny eyes daring the witch to make a sudden move.

I tried to step toward them but my legs didn't hold me up. Quinn trailed concern across my face, searching for some answer that I didn't have, and tightened his hold around me.

"You okay?" he asked, though the question must surely have been rhetorical. Clearly I wasn't. "Can I carry you to the couch?"

I was used to being the proverbial runt of the litter. The entirety of the Kunu Clan, even my mother and Liana on occasion, had treated me as if I were weaker and in need of constant assistance. But I'd resisted their efforts and had never allowed a single one of them to carry my burdens.

But when I met Quinn's eyes I didn't find judgment, no thoughts that I was weak or less than.

I swallowed my pride, but realized that with this shifter I didn't need to. Finally, I nodded my assent, and even that effort left my head swimming.

Things were going splendidly. Since I'd crossed the threshold into Irving's home, I'd almost died at least once, and it sure felt like it'd been twice. And that was *before* the vampires, shifters, ghouls, ghosts, undead, and whatever other ghastly creature they'd managed to recruit to their cause of world domination caught up with me.

"You…" Fianna growled at Naomi.

"I didn't do this," the witch said. "Think it through, dummy. There's no reason for me to try to kill Selene. I couldn't even do it if I wanted to thanks to the binding you supervised."

"Don't you call me dummy, dummy."

"Don't be one, and I won't."

"Lasses, I mean it," Irving said, and from the tone of his voice it was clear that he did. "I'll expel you from here in the next five seconds if ya don't pipe down and holster your magic."

Quinn crouched, and in one sweep I was in his arms, pressed against his chest, my wings hanging from behind his arm.

"Take it easy," Irving said to his nephew. "Really slow."

I wanted to tell him I wasn't made of porcelain, but the truth was I felt as if I'd shatter if Naomi did a single bit more of … well, whatever it was she'd done.

The fairies glared at Naomi instead of watching Quinn's progress with me. Fianna bit out, "Drop your magic and we will." But she said it more softly, as if she realized Irving was really about to kick them all out.

Naomi didn't respond for long enough that Irving turned toward her. When he did, she let the green between her hands fizzle out to nothing, but the look on her face made it abundantly clear she was ready to munch on tiny fairies and pick her teeth with their bones after.

"Watch yourself," Irving said, and I suspected there was much more to that warning than I realized. It was enough for Naomi to wipe the menacing snarl from her face and stash it away—for later use, no doubt.

Fianna and Nessa allowed the light that coursed between their hands to fade out before Irving could give them the stink-eye, though Fianna didn't stop glaring at the witch for a second.

Quinn went to lay me down on the couch so that I could stretch out across it lengthwise, belatedly remembered I had unwieldy wings attached to my back, and helped me sit instead.

I yelped as my wings pulled in the wrong direction when he draped them across the back of the couch.

He stilled immediately, hovering over me. "I'm so sorry. How do I fix it?"

"No, it's fine. I just … hurt all over."

Quinn nodded and fully released my weight to the couch. When he stood, Irving gave him a look that said, *We need to talk*. Before I properly anticipated what I was going to say, I said it: "Please stay with me." I directed my words to both of them, but I really meant Quinn.

He didn't wait for his uncle's permission, but sat down next to me on the couch without a word. Tension I hadn't even noticed I was still carrying left my body as I felt his warmth. I sank into the couch.

I hoped he didn't think it was strange that we'd only just met and already I was becoming reliant on him. Once I figured things out a little, I wouldn't allow myself to depend on him or anyone else like this.

I avoided his searching gaze when I felt it land on

me. I looked instead to Irving. I needed answers, lots of them.

"What happened to me?" I croaked, and hurried to clear my throat so I wouldn't sound so weak. "Was it the wards again?" What I really wanted to ask was if Naomi had tried to kill me somehow. Had she found some loophole in the binding? I didn't dare upset the witch.

Irving looked to Naomi, who shook her head, actually appearing sincere for once. "It wasn't anything I did. And it wasn't the wards, I'm sure of it. I was connected to them. I would have sensed some kind of deviation from the rules I set for them. The wards are working exactly as they're supposed to."

"It has to have been the wards," Irving said. "Nothing else makes sense."

"Maybe it was my power that activated whatever happened, but it wasn't anything I did on purpose."

When no one offered their agreement right away, she added, "You can be sure of what I'm saying because of the binding. I can't have set out to hurt our newest hybrid, now could I?"

"Fianna?" Irving asked.

The crimson fairy sighed heavily. "It wasn't on purpose. Whatever happened to Selene was because of the witch's powers, but not because she was trying to hurt her." Fianna grimaced as if that were bad news instead of good.

"You have to check with the fairy before you trust me?" Naomi asked, narrowing her eyes at the gruff shifter.

"Yes," Irving said. "But I don't fully trust either of you, if that makes ya happy."

I didn't think Naomi knew how to be happy, not in the real sense. Victorious, yes. Happy, no way.

"You should trust me," Naomi said.

"I'd be happy to. But trust is earned. Are the wards in place now?"

Naomi nodded. "Perfectly. They'll no longer hurt Selene, but they'll fry anyone who attempts to enter this house without permission."

"I assume you made a back entrance for you to come and go as you please."

Naomi blinked, the only sign of her surprise. "Well done, old man."

I expected another one of Irving's threats not to call him old, but he didn't mention it. "We'll deal with that later. Now that we're protected, we need to get to business. Not a second to waste. Are creatures still coming for her?"

"Undoubtedly." Naomi's response was too quick for my liking. "I sense shifters and vamps clearly now. Their energy signatures are so distinct for me. They're close, and they aren't alone."

Great. The day just kept getting better.

"What else is with them?" Irving asked.

"Hmm, I still can't tell. It's … muddled."

"Like they might have a witch working to conceal their approach?" Nessa asked.

"Yes, that might be it." Naomi dragged the words out.

"If they're working with witches, that's really bad," Quinn said. "We need to protect Selene."

"We absolutely do," Irving said, "but first we need to figure out what happened just now. We can't have her reacting to magic like that. We could accidentally kill her."

I nodded fervently, making myself a bit dizzy. I was all for not getting killed on my first day on land.

"Does anyone have any ideas?" Irving asked, pacing across the open length of the room all the way to the sliding glass door. The thick, corded muscles of his forearms rippled with tension. "Because I've never seen anything like that before."

"Nor have I," Naomi said. "No one's ever reacted to my magic like that. Then again, I've never worked magic that accounted for a siren angel."

"A sirangel," Nessa said, most unhelpfully.

"Do ya think it's that her powers are different and new?" Irving asked. "Could that have been it? Reacting to magic on land that she's never been exposed to before?"

"Possible, but unlikely. No, I think it has to have been more than that. Something we aren't taking into account." Naomi's eyes widened and she sank back into the armchair, ramrod straight in the seat. She pinned all her attention on Quinn and me over on the couch. I wanted to squirm to escape it, but I suddenly sensed that it was important not to reveal any more of my weaknesses to this woman.

I met her gaze without flinching, even though my

insides were going all wonky from the effort, and I was already light-headed to begin with.

I'd have to work at it.

"Nessa the Sapphire?" Irving asked. "Do you have any thoughts on this?"

"Nessa always has thoughts on the matter," Fianna said.

Nessa tilted her head and looked at Quinn and me. With her attention, everyone else followed. I struggled to keep from showing the effort it took not to hide from their gazes. I wanted to burrow my face into Quinn's chest and let the worries of the world fall away—if only that were possible.

"There's definitely more to it than Selene's magic encountering Naomi's for the first time," Nessa said. "Though that might be part of it. Naomi has strong magic, but since it wasn't targeted at Selene, it has to have been something more."

Nessa buzzed her wings into a blur behind her and flew over to Quinn and me, where she hovered right between our faces, and I had to resist the automatic urge to shoo an annoying, buzzing pest from my face.

She got so close that I struggled not to blink as she stared into my eyes, then flew over to Quinn's and stared into his. "Hmm," she said, and flew back to peer into my eyes again. "Ah-ha, yes, I suspected it must be something like this."

"Something like what?" Quinn asked.

But Nessa addressed Irving. "You never told us about Quinn."

"I had no reason to. I only just met you."

"And he's your nephew to protect."

"Of course. There's that too. And it's the reason why I'm not going to tell ya a thing now either."

Nessa smiled, and it was both regretful and triumphant. "There's no need. I already know. The eyes reveal everything the person is reluctant to say."

Irving ceased his pacing and squared his shoulders as if to face an invisible foe. "Yes, I've found that to be the case. If y'already know, fine. But ya can't say anything about it to anyone outside of this circle, and ya have to promise. All of you do."

"And what of Naomi?" Fianna asked. "You trust the witch. Oh."

"Right, I've had to—"

"For her to be able to complete the protective wards and include him in their protection."

Irving nodded.

Fianna frowned at the witch. "You know, I think witches do that on purpose, to learn everyone's little secrets."

Naomi's mauve lips spread into a wicked grin. "Every witch has to have her secrets."

"And as many of everyone else's as they can get their greedy hands on."

Naomi didn't apologize. "We deal in power, as, might I add, do the fairies."

Fianna didn't say anything. They'd reached an impasse, and the grandfather clock on the wall was counting down the approach of my faceless enemies.

Quinn's eyes were swimming with emotion, which

meant he either knew what this big secret was, or he suspected.

Nessa said, "We fairies promise not to reveal the secret of Quinn's … makeup, shall we say? And we fairies keep our promises." Nessa's chest swelled in pride.

My breath caught in my chest, and I forgot that I was weak from whatever happened. Alertness swept across my body, leaving it tight. I trained my eyes on Quinn, who struggled to meet mine, as he stared at where his hand touched my leg.

Whatever this secret was, it was big.

"Quinn here is also a hybrid," said Nessa. "Just like Selene."

✿ 12 ✿

I GASPED SO VIOLENTLY THAT I CHOKED. "WHAT?" I finally managed to croak out while waving Nessa away so I'd have some space to choke in peace.

No one bothered repeating what Nessa said. We'd all heard her.

Quinn finally met my eyes, which watered from the air I'd sucked down the wrong pipe. "It's true," he said.

"Why do you sound so sad when you say it?" There were far more useful questions, but his lament was terribly heavy.

He opened his mouth to answer, but didn't seem to know what to say. "I just ... I don't know. It hasn't been easy." He shrugged and looked away, once more unwilling to meet my probing gaze.

"Well, I definitely understand 'not easy.' Nothing is easy when you're different."

"Not different in a bad way, remember?" Nessa said. "Special is good."

But neither Quinn nor I did anything to agree. I'd wished I was just like the other sirens a million times at least, and like one of the mermaids a thousand times. I'd been willing to give up the power of my song if only it meant I wouldn't have to be the odd one out for once.

"Yes, well, we don't need to focus on any of this now," Irving said, his tone firm and urgent, setting nerves aflutter in my chest all over again. "No one needs to know any more details about Quinn unless they directly pertain to our surviving the day."

My heart rate picked up. The shifter didn't sound as hopeful as I would have liked.

"Sure, I get it," Fianna said, "but it seems you've already forgotten what just went down in your desire to protect your nephew." Irving's bushy mustache twitched. "Naomi's magic, while not directed at the girl or boy, almost killed her. And there's no denying there's some kind of connection between the two of them. You say they just met, and yet look at them."

Five heads swiveled in our direction.

"They can't stand to be apart from each other already," Fianna said.

I fiddled with my short skirt, tugging it down my thighs, while Quinn pulled his hand away from my leg. Our closeness was my fault. I was weak, just as I'd always been, and Quinn responded to my weakness. His instinct was to protect, not to connect.

"Of course they can be apart," Irving said. "Don't be ridiculous. Selene only arrived a couple of hours ago."

When Quinn didn't rise from the couch to prove his uncle's point, and I did nothing to encourage it, a cloud swept across Irving's stormy eyes. "Well, anyway, what does any of that have to do with those hunting Selene?" But I could tell Irving hadn't actually dismissed Fianna's point, he only behaved as if he had. "The matter is urgent, dammit," he barked.

"Which is precisely why we need to understand what we're dealing with," Nessa said with the patience of a scholar no one else possessed. "Their connection is obviously unnatural."

"Unnatural?" Quinn protested.

Nessa waved her tiny hand unconcernedly and touched down on the table next to the fairies' abandoned teacups. "Special. An uncommon connection." She batted her eyelashes, blinking cerulean eyes at Quinn. "Now that we've discovered you're both special, and Naomi's magic almost killed Selene, though you were there to save her from it, we can't dismiss the power of your connection."

"That's assuming there even is any kind of power from this ... connection," Irving said, and Nessa pointed a "come-on" look at him.

"Your nephew's connected to this girl. Deal with it," she said.

"But if that's the case, it would put him in danger."

"Perhaps. Or it could be the exact opposite. You know as well as we do that powers combine in unusual ways. There's never been a sirangel before, and this one isn't activated. She has no clue about the extent of her powers, no idea what she's capable of. It's only just beginning for her. Heck, she doesn't even know how to fly yet, let alone access whatever powers she might've inherited from her father. From the looks of her, she probably doesn't even know what she can do with her siren magic."

I plastered an offended look on my face, even though everything she said was absolutely true.

Nessa didn't even bother looking at me. "What about the boy? Does he have access to the full range of his powers?"

"I don't," Quinn answered, before Irving could speak for him. "Uncle has forbidden it." The bitterness of the denial was blatant.

Fianna moved next to Nessa on the table across from the couch to join her in staring at us—up close and personal—while Irving tilted his chin upward. "I did what I had to do to protect ya, child. If ya'd activated your full powers, the hunters would've arrived ages ago, and then what would be of ya?"

"I don't even know what kind of hybrid I am."

I gasped and spun to face Quinn.

"Yeah, I know," Quinn said, heat blazing in his eyes, making the different colors in his irises dance. "I don't even know what brand of freak I am."

"Q!" Irving said.

He was as bitter as a lime. "Whatever, Uncle. I get it, same as I always have. Protect poor, strange Q. I'm used to it. Don't you worry."

Irving fumed, but I didn't think at Quinn's

outburst. No, they'd been through this many times before.

"Jeez, the drama," Naomi said, though her greedy smirk indicated that she loved it, probably fed on the misery of others. "Snap to, creatures. Vamps and shifters are on their way, possibly with a whole horde of minions."

"Right," Fianna said. "Until we figure things out better, we should probably separate the girl and the boy."

My breath hitched painfully. Quinn tensed and slid closer to me under the guise of adjusting his position on the couch. The entirety of his leg pressed against mine, and I wished his pants weren't in the way of feeling his skin.

"I need to help protect Selene," he said, and every part inside of me sang out in agreement.

"Those hunters are coming for a new hybrid, not specifically Selene," Irving said. "Sure, they'll go into power lust when they discover she's a sirangel, but they won't leave you behind. Ya'll be valuable to them too."

"I don't care."

"I do, and ya'll do what I say."

"The days of you barking orders at me are over. I'm eighteen, and so is she. That's majority of age for all shifters, even the 'special' ones like us. I'm staying with Selene, and that's the end of the discussion."

Breath flowed easily again. It was true, our connection was unnatural—magical. It made no sense that I should panic at the thought of this near stranger leaving my side.

"You're one of a kind too, son, just as much as she is," Irving persisted. "The hunters will want ya too."

Quinn stiffened. "You never told me that, and I'm not your son, or you wouldn't have kept something so big from me."

Irving's nostrils flared like an animal's, and again I found myself desperate to figure out what he shifted into. "You're just like a son, dammit. Now get your head out of your arse and listen to me. There's no other hybrid out there like ya."

"Well, I guess I'll have to take your word for it since I don't even know what the hell I am."

"How could he not know?" Fianna asked Nessa, and Quinn whipped his head toward her. "Selene and I are right here. You don't have to keep talking about us like we belong in some lab tank. I don't know because Uncle never told me. Nor did he allow me to figure it out on my own. I've been a prisoner of this house."

Irving chuffed. "Ya have not."

"Fine, of this house and the yard."

"I own fifty acres for you to roam. That's not exactly confining, now is it?"

"Again with the drama…" Naomi said. "At this rate, you'll be all trussed up and waiting for the hunters coming your way. They're almost upon us."

Irving nodded quickly. "Q, this is no time to argue. You head out into the woods, as far from here as ya can get. Naomi's wards extend that far." Irving looked to the witch for confirmation and she nodded. "You'll be safer the farther away from

Selene ya get. The hunters won't go looking for you in the woods."

"And what of Selene?" Quinn asked.

"We'll all protect her, obviously."

"You have no idea what's coming or how many. Naomi and the fairies don't owe her any loyalty. Neither do you, by the way."

"I owe her a duty. Mulunu's called in a debt, and I intend to pay up." When Quinn just stared at him, he added, "If anything to get the old bag off my back. Nobody wants to owe a sea witch like Mulunu a damn thing. I've been waiting ten years for her to collect."

"Ten years?" Quinn asked. "Does she have anything to do with—?"

"Enough with the questions. You get the hell out of here, ya hear me?" Irving stomped across the room and stopped in front of us, on the other side of the table. His entire face quivered beneath his beard. He was afraid—not for himself but for Quinn.

"Uncle—"

"You're fast. You run as far as ya can get, and you don't come back no matter what ya hear or see, you got me?"

"I won't leave Selene. You talk of this connection we have—"

"I haven't said a word about it. It's been everyone else muddying the waters. You need to get out before it's too late."

Quinn looked to me, those multi-colored eyes that ranged from yellow to green to blue meeting my own. "I can't."

"Of course ya can," Irving roared. "Get your butt in motion, boy."

"No, you don't understand me, *I can't*. I have to be here to help her. I can't explain it, but I feel it."

I nodded slowly. I felt it too, though I didn't understand it any better than he appeared to.

Fianna flew to hover above our forgotten teacups. "You have to go, Quinn. If you stay, and Selene's in danger, her magic will likely flare, and remember that we have no idea what the powers of a sirangel might do. Your magic will almost certainly come to the surface to protect her since something binds you two together. Your magic is as unexplored and potentially unstable as hers. We've already seen what happens when a witch's magic interferes with her powers. Under attack, what if one of your powers hurts the other? You won't know how to control yourselves." The red-haired fairy paused for effect, her wings buzzing quietly behind her. "What if one of you kills the other?"

My breath caught and I brought a hand to my chest, my heart thumping beneath my touch. "We can't risk that, not for anything."

"And if I leave and something hurts or kills you because I'm not here to protect you?" Quinn asked. He didn't appear embarrassed at the sentiment no matter that we'd just met. He must feel the connection as strongly as I did.

"If I accidentally kill you, I'll never forgive myself, and you don't want me to live with that burden."

"Just as you don't want me to live with the burden

of leaving and having something happen to you." he said.

"Enough with the googly eyes," Naomi snapped. "Quinn, you take that pretty behind of yours and make it move so fast it blurs. Selene, you stick close to me. I'll make sure you two meet again and all that sticky nonsense."

Neither Quinn nor I moved.

"Now!" she barked, making me jump. "They're almost here. I can feel them approaching. If they find out there are two one-of-a-kind hybrids here, you'll make their decade. If they discover the hybrids are connected someway, they won't just drain you of your powers, they won't stop until they've figured out what makes you tick, and what happens when you tick together. They'll push you until you're as dead and heartless as they are, do you hear me?"

Of course I did; she was practically yelling. I nodded, unable to say a word, and Quinn squeezed my hand. His was so much warmer than mine, so reassuring.

"Go!" Naomi roared again, while Fianna nodded her agreement, her red head bopping. Nessa fussed with her skirt, her little brows drawn and her mouth puckered in worry.

Irving clapped a hand to Quinn's shoulder. "Come back in one piece, ya hear me, my boy? I'll call for ya. You know how."

Quinn nodded, and his eyes that dripped with concern met mine one last time. I wanted to freeze that moment forever. I trailed a desperate gaze across every one of his features, working to memorize the precise slant of his eyebrows, cheeks, and lips. The width of his shoulders, the exact temperature of his skin, the shade of his dark hair. I tried to make sense of the many colors that swirled in his irises, to coalesce them into a single color I could hold on to.

But Irving grabbed his free hand and yanked him up off the couch. Quinn's hand slipped from mine and I experienced his absence as a physical pain that carved a jagged path all the way from my hand to my heart. Irving shoved him across the floor, toward the back door, while Quinn craned his neck to look at me.

Then, with a swoosh of the sliding-glass door, the only person who'd helped me feel safe was gone.

"Prepare yourselves," Naomi said. "They're nearly upon us."

I could barely breathe.

❧ 13 ❧

"THEY'RE NOT NEARLY UPON US. THEY'RE HERE!"
Fianna shouted. "Call the kid back, old man. There's
no time for him to hide where they won't find him."

Panic swept across Irving as it did me, but the "old
man" got right to it, shoving the sliding-glass door
back open and racing outside with all the agility and
strength of youth.

I didn't know what to do to help. I launched
myself to standing, tore at my wings, winced at the
sting of it, but then had nothing to do but fidget and
frantically scan the room.

The fairies were speaking among themselves,
intent on preparing our defense, I hoped, and Naomi
had already ignited her powers. A bright green glow
surrounded her; sparks the vibrant color of moss
crackled across her skin. "Come on, come on," she
muttered.

Breathing became difficult as the moments
stretched and neither Irving nor Quinn returned.

"Petunia," Naomi scolded, looking at nothing in particular. "Get your furry butt over here right now."

I gaped at the crazy witch. There was no one with a furry butt around.

"Please," she added, when I hadn't believed she was familiar with the word, still speaking to the empty air in front of her.

But then the time to figure out the witch and what she could possibly be doing ended with a bang.

A force as strong as the ocean itself pounded against the house. Walls and ceiling thumped. I sucked in a breath and waited to see if it'd all fall in around us.

The house expanded back outward with a terrifying groan and the glass in every window in the sitting room shattered. Glass shards flew everywhere, both inside and out, in an explosion that set my ears to ringing.

I crouched and partially shielded myself with the tea table, spreading my wings along the skin of my back, mostly bare around my sleeveless crop top, to protect it. The teacups rattled and wobbled in large arcs upon their saucers, and the cream pitcher imploded, launching large shards of porcelain and splatters of cream at me.

I screamed, sure no one would hear me over the din, and yanked a wedge-shaped piece of pitcher from my forearm like it was on fire and I had to get it out fast. I couldn't give myself time to think on it or I'd freak out. The porcelain shard was thick and left a deep, bleeding gash the size of my pinky finger. I grabbed one of the fairies' discarded cloth napkins, only slightly damp after they'd toweled off following their baths, wrapped it around my forearm and tied it tight with my teeth. There, that was all I could do, and I was certain it was to be the least of my problems.

I felt the next attack coming as if the undertow of the sea were sucking back only to crest forward with more force. I whimpered and curled into the smallest shape I could, wrapping my wings around myself to also encompass most of my bare legs. Maybe that wasn't smart; maybe the next blast would rent my wings from my back. But cocooned inside my wings I was able to pretend that I wasn't in a nightmare. Thrust on land against my will, I was under attack, and the only good point to come of all of it was somewhere outside, probably fighting for his life along with Irving … if he'd managed to survive the initial onslaught of the hunters' magic that was strong enough to rattle a house.

"Petunia!" Naomi yelled in the terrifying moment before the second attack arrived.

It was just my luck to have the witch, and perhaps our greatest chance at surviving this assault, lose her mind right when the hunters got here.

Thwump! The air seemed to suck out of the house, fleeing through the bare windows.

"Hurry," a tiny voice said across the room, but at its frantic pitch I couldn't tell which of the fairies it was.

The house sucked all the air back in as if it were reaching for its dying breath. My ears popped at the sudden shift in air pressure, altering the pitch of the constant ringing in them.

A fissure as wide as my arm tore down the wall that divided sitting room from entryway. Like a lightning bolt it struck, searing the wall as it went. This wasn't just any force, this was magic, and it sizzled as it swept through the house that was supposed to be invulnerable thanks to Naomi's wards. From what the witch had said, I'd understood that the hunters shouldn't have even been able to enter the fifty acres that enclosed Irving's house. Either her wards weren't as strong as she believed them to be, or the hunters were far more powerful than she'd anticipated. Either option was bad news.

"Finally," Naomi said, again to air that was empty except for the fine particles of plaster raining down from the trembling ceiling. "You took long enough. We'll have to address your response time later."

Great. We were in the middle of an invasion and the witch was having conversations with an imaginary … Petunia.

Another rattling thump and the floor beneath my bare feet shook, building strength like an earthquake. Even my thoughts shook loose from my mind as my entire body vibrated, my long hair shaking around my down-turned face. I placed my palms flat on the floor in search of any kind of stability. Of course that didn't help. The constant motion of the house made me dizzy, as if I were caught in the undertow of the ocean, desperate for stillness.

"Petunia, now!" Naomi yelled, drawing my attention to her once more. The witch had seemed intelligent and meticulous, conniving even. Her outbursts made no sense. Could the magic of these hunters outside the house be affecting her somehow?

A wave of bright green energy blasted out from Naomi ... and a speckled cat was then perched on her shoulder, where it barely fit. The cat's eyes blazed the exact color green as Naomi's magic.

I blinked, trying to understand what I was seeing. Where the heck had that cat come from?

Then Naomi's magic barreled against me, pushing with enough force to knock me off my feet. I landed on my butt atop pieces of Irving's destroyed dainty tea set. I brushed my wings out from under me and popped back up to a crouch.

"Again," Naomi said to the cat, who sat on her slim shoulder.

From behind them, as the dust settled enough to see across the room, I finally caught sight of the fairies. Fianna shot wave after wave of crimson magic at the ceiling and walls, while Nessa sent her sapphire magic flinging right after it, though at a slower pace. Nessa's mouth moved a league a minute as she released her magic and immediately worked to rebuild it. It appeared that the fairies were working to fortify the house, or maybe the witch's wards—both were obviously needed.

A green, crackling glow swept out from Naomi to encompass her and her cat. The witch brought her hands in front of her, and I ran for the entryway before another one of her blasts could knock me on my ass. As soon as I exited the sitting area, I plastered myself against the wall that faced the other side.

The house thumped again, and this time I was in position to see the front door stretch against its hinges. It expanded like a long strand of kelp before shrinking back to its normal size. Surely they must be magical hinges. No wood or brass stretched that far without breaking.

But even if some spell fortified the doorway, how much longer could it hold? The house was threatening to fall apart at the seams.

"Where's the girl?" I heard Naomi call out to the fairies.

"I don't know!" Fianna yelled. "Nessa, find her."

I ran back toward the sitting area. No need to distract them from whatever they were doing, which was probably actually helpful, as opposed to the freaking out I was mostly doing.

Nessa slammed straight into my face. I swatted before realizing I shouldn't, and sneezed when the fairy's azure hair tickled my nose. My sneeze sent her shooting off in the opposite direction, so I dove to catch her because I thought she was falling.

"Get away from me," Nessa said, stumbling in flight but catching herself, twisting to brush my hands away before I could touch her. "Good grief, girl, stop swiping at me."

"Sorry," I said, then grit my teeth. Every single piece of me vibrated as the house shook and struggled to remain more or less in one piece.

Nessa's eyes widened and she looked around us,

taking in the growing damage to our supposedly safe refuge. "You're not going to hit me again, right?"

"Of course not. I didn't mean to in the first place. I just reacted. I don't know what to do."

"Use your powers, obviously," the blue fairy said in her battle wear. "We're under attack."

Well, duh. "I don't really have any powers," I said, in my barely-there clothing that matched my total lack of preparation for our defense.

"You must. Every magical creature does. And you're a sirangel."

"But—"

"Figure it out," she snapped as she pointed herself back in the direction of Fianna, who continued to shoot off red magic at the house without her. "And stay where we can see you!" Nessa called over her tiny shoulder.

I crept along the outermost edge of the sitting area and pressed myself against the wall, until a fissure large enough to pull me into it shattered that wall as well. I squealed, realized belatedly that I'd distract the fairies and witch working to defend me, and clamped my mouth shut.

Use my powers, Nessa had told me, but clearly she didn't realize that I really meant it when I said I didn't have any. Not in any real sense. I was a siren, or at least half of one. I was the daughter of the most powerful siren our clan had; her powers were second only to Mulunu's, who wasn't a siren. Her song was so strong that she had managed to woo an angel when angels were supposedly impervious to the influences of Earth and her oceans.

But just because my mother's song was strong didn't mean I'd inherited the scope of her skill. And just because I was the daughter of an angel didn't mean I could do whatever angels did. I knew next to nothing of my father, no matter how much I defended him. He was no more than a picture in my mind, borne from my mother's repeated stories of their love.

The next slap against the house tore at the ceiling until plaster showered down from above like a rainstorm. I coughed and wheezed as I breathed in the dust, reaching for the wall to hold myself up. The house was crumbling around us, and that was despite Naomi's wards and all of her present efforts and the fairies'. Worst of all, my presence was what had brought this chaos on everyone else ... and Quinn and Irving were out there somewhere, without even the protection of the house.

Quinn. I had to see him again, I just had to.

I stopped panicking, I stopped thinking, and I just opened my mouth.

I usually had to set an intention for the course of my song, but I was too unsettled for that. The house was now falling in big chunks and dissolving into powdery pieces.

I sang, surprised at how different my song sounded outside of the water. I hesitated at the unfamiliar pitch, cleared my throat, then forced myself along.

I released my water magic in whatever direction it wanted to go, to do whatever it could do to save us. I gathered strength and confidence, and sang, managing to forget a bit about my crumbling surroundings and lose myself to the tune and melody. I didn't know if my song would accomplish anything useful, but at least it was already calming me.

I pulled my top up to cover my mouth and breathed in as deeply as I could through the fabric, filling my lungs, and then belted out a tune that possessed none of the worry ratcheting through my body. I unfurled my wings fully and allowed my shoulders to relax despite the foreign feeling. I sang as my attention hazily traveled to the sliding-glass door.

The song died on my lips with a strangled sound.

I wrapped my wings around myself again to hide. But it was too late.

❧ 14 ❧

IF THERE WAS SOMETHING USEFUL I COULD HAVE DONE
when the vampire looked through the sliding-glass
door across the room at me, I couldn't imagine it then.
I gaped at him from an opening between my wings
until I realized I shouldn't make it obvious how easy
of a target I was—though that ship had probably
sailed, let's be real.

I'd never seen a vampire before, but I had no
doubt that's what the man, who wasn't quite a man,
was. He was too pretty and his features too perfect to
be an average human. Though he hadn't spoken a
single word to me, nor gestured in any way, my heart
thumped loudly, dangerously so—he could probably
hear my erratic heartbeat across the distance that
separated us. A dark, goopy energy—his magic probably—rolled off him like waves. When it hit me, the
flashes of green, red, and blue magic of my allies
faded to the background, along with their shouts and
the chaos. All I could focus on was him; he made my

stomach roll with nausea strong enough that I wondered if I might hurl in front of him and make the announcement of my vulnerability complete.

His hair was dark as midnight under a new moon. His eyes, somehow, were even darker; their pupils disappeared into the black of his irises. Tall, his body lithe and strong, he was a consummate predator.

I swallowed with difficulty, and his perfect full lips stretched into a deadly grin. Even across the room, I sensed him as if he were right next to me, breathing down my neck, promising pain—or possibly pain disguised as pleasure. I stumbled backward until my wings and back met the wall, his dark magic rolling over me so tangibly that I snapped a quick look to either side to confirm he wasn't somehow next to me.

He wasn't inside the house, of course. He couldn't be ... yet. When my gaze traveled across the devastation of the sitting room toward him again, he flicked his tongue from his mouth, then ran it seductively across his bright lips, so slowly that I couldn't help but follow the movement. My breath hitched as his tongue finished its slow sweep.

He grinned, his smile as deadly as everything else about him, revealing elongating fangs.

What, was I to be a late lunch? I thought the vamps wanted my magic, not my blood. Maybe they wanted both. I squirmed against the wall and willed myself not to whimper. Were Quinn and Irving out there battling others like this vampire? Would the two shifters survive if they were? Quinn had never even shifted before.

This vampire was a shark, at the top of the food chain, and his sights were set on me. Hiding behind my wings was a futile gesture. With regret, I slowly pulled back the partial curtains they formed in front of me.

I should have protected the secret of my true nature with my life, yet I'd revealed it to a predator hunting me for my uniqueness. The vampire had heard me singing, and there was no way he'd confuse my siren's song for anything else. Even if my song hadn't swayed him, he'd surely identified it for what it was. The way it vibrated through the body and pushed against the heart and mind, a siren's song felt like so much more than music. The undead would experience that too, even if their hearts no longer beat. A vampire as evidently capable as this one would recognize magic, certainly.

I stashed my wings away as well as I could and met the vampire's probing gaze. I shouldn't reveal weakness. This creature thrived on fear. If I let mine out, he'd feast on it for a week.

No, it was time to pretend I was something I wasn't.

I squared my shoulders and imagined wings didn't hang from them. I met his gaze head-on and refused to look away although my insides protested at the effort. What I wanted to do—desperately —was run.

The vampire's body flickered for an instant before solidifying outside the sliding-glass door again. And another time. He disappeared for a fraction of a second before materializing in the same spot. What the heck?

A third time his body vanished … and this time it shimmered into existence right next to me. I screeched and jumped away from him, my heart in my throat. But when I landed, he was gone.

I whipped my head back around to the sliding-glass door. He was there again, his eyes narrowed at me.

"I'll get in there soon enough," he said, his voice a terrifying combination of seduction and deadly promise. "The witch's wards won't protect you forever. No witch is powerful enough to take me on. Eventually, you'll be mine. And so will your power." His lips crept upward, exposing long, shiny fangs. "All of you will be mine."

I shivered. It was clear he believed himself capable of delivering on his promises. "No," I said to the vampire, and even that short word shook my voice. "You won't take me." If he hadn't been a vampire, he might not have heard me over the cacophony of witch and fairies defending against the magical equivalent of tsunamis this vampire's compatriots were hurling against the house.

But this vampire made out every word I said, even when all I had in me was a whisper.

"You won't ever have me or my power," I said.

He responded by shimmering again. This time when he popped up right next to me, he lingered for several seconds longer, and his outstretched fingers caressed my forearm where the creamer pitcher had cut me. His touch was as cold as arctic water.

I froze, unable to move until he was gone again. The house was shaking in non-stop protests of the violence of the assault. It wouldn't hold much longer, and the moment Naomi's wards failed entirely, the vampire would be inside. He'd take me. There'd be nothing I could do to stop him.

I looked toward Naomi, her cat, and the fairies, all congregated in the middle of the room yelling spells and shooting wave after wave of magic toward the interior of the house. They fought our attackers by reinforcing the only defense that stood between us and them. They hadn't even noticed the vampire who'd nearly managed to slip through the wards.

I forced my magic to rise to the occasion. Dammit, I had no better choice. The vampire was already flickering again from outside the empty panes of the sliding-glass door. How long would it be before he managed to remain inside the house long enough to pull me outside along with him? Like with any creature, the magical abilities of vampires varied. If this one could get through Naomi's wards when nothing else yet could, I shouldn't underestimate him. Though I'd never experienced the entirety of my magic, surely it could do something to help me survive.

He materialized inside the house again, and the shark-who-ate-the-seal look he gave me threatened to crush my spirit before he reappeared outside the empty doorway again. Then he finally trailed his gaze from mine to the sliding doorframe in front of him.

"I'm coming for you," he promised, reaching a hand toward the vacant doorframe, moving slowly. There was nothing between the vampire and me but air—and hopefully a protective ward still strong enough to withstand his magic.

He pinned his unnerving stare back on me. I stopped breathing entirely and pressed my arms against the wall behind me. His hand was already inside the house, past the first knuckle.

My stomach fell. The wards had failed and now he'd come for me. Magic, I had to spark my magic somehow. I had to do something, anything.

He thrust his whole hand inside.

His flesh sizzled and melted, skin peeling from the bone in angry, red strips. His eyes tightened and he withdrew his hand quickly, little more than a blur, hissing at the damage. But he didn't even spare a glance at his hand, which began to heal quickly—too quickly. If his healing magic was this advanced, maybe not even Naomi could stop him if—when—her wards fell.

Something zipped in front of my face, and I screamed and shrank against the wall, thinking the vampire was there to get me.

"What are you doing?" Nessa shouted at me, buzzing at eye level. Her hair was covered in white plaster, muting its cerulean color, and her eyes were feverish, wild. "What are you thinking?" Hands on hips, she glared at me. "You don't play footsie with a vamp!" She turned to shoot the vamp a death glare.

When she turned back to me, she whispered, "They always win."

Movement behind her drew my attention back to the vamp. His grin was wide enough to split his too-handsome face. If he'd heard Nessa's tinkly whispers, then there was nowhere safe to speak within the house.

"Come on. Move," the fairy admonished, getting my leaden feet to take me out of the vampire's line of sight.

Even desperate to get away from him, it was diffi-cult to resist the urge to turn back to look at him some more. Humans must have no hope against vampires. The vamp's eyes were mesmerizing, and though they suggested torment, they also whispered promises of pleasure. I imagined even a vampire as threatening as this one could be irresistibly enchanting if he so desired. It only made him all the more dangerous.

Nessa hovered next to my ear and whispered so that the vampire wouldn't hear over the din, "Don't let him see he has power over you. Vamps feed on that stuff."

"Yeah, I gathered that," I said, half there, half entranced by the vamp. A sharp yank tore at my ear. "Ow! What'd you do that for?"

The little fairy shook her head at me in blatant disappointment. "We need to train you, stat, or we're all going to be in big trouble."

I half turned and she bit out, "Don't you dare turn back around. Get your heiny over next to Naomi and that blasted cat of hers and stay there. No matter what you see, you don't look, you hear me?"

"Loud and clear."

"Good." She huffed and shook out her hands to the sound of bells. I searched for the source of the melody but didn't find it. "Now I've got to save Fianna's behind *again*. And when it's all said and done, she'll say she saved me instead—again. You just wait and see." She sighed her torment, then flitted off to join the others. I hurried after her to remain close.

Fianna's crimson hair stood in all different directions; plaster smudged her face and clothes. But the grimace on her face was determined and fierce as she shot blast after blast of red, sparkling magic at the walls and ceilings. Her magic coated the inside of the house, spreading across every visible surface in a thick layer of glowing scarlet. Nessa flittered to her side and started chanting another spell until blue light erupted from her palms.

Maybe the fairies could teach me how to do that…

"What are you doing, girl?" Naomi barked at me as she held a beam of green energy in both palms, connecting the floor and ceiling with it. I snapped my head toward her. "There's no time to gape about like you have no more than two brain cells to rub together. Get to doing something helpful before my wards fail and the entire damn house comes crashing down at us." Her cat screeched and jumped as a clump of plaster fell on her.

"Wh-what exactly should I do? I tried magic and that only got me in trouble with a vamp." It was technically true. Even though I'd sung for less than a minute, it'd been enough to deliver me to the vamp's hungry attention.

Naomi's astute gaze whipped toward the sliding door. I looked too, disobeying Nessa, but the vamp was no longer there. Ah, so the witch had sensed the vampire there after all.

She scowled. "Nothing to do about that now. We'll deal with whatever you did later. Now it's time for all your powers." She refocused her attention on the magic she streamed from her hands.

"But that's what revealed who I was to the vamp earlier," I complained.

Her head whipped back around to me so fast that clumps of hair ended up in her eyes; she blew out the side of her mouth and flicked her head to clear them. Then her light eyes seared through me. "The vamp knows *what* you are?"

I shrugged under the weight of her stare, ready to jump out of my skin. I was more than happy to leave my legs and wings behind, as long as I got to leave all the trouble behind too.

"Dammit." She shook her head violently, her blond bob far from perfect now, and cursed up a storm like a sailor. She flicked her hands and the green magic fizzled to nothing. Petunia leapt onto her shoulder in a single bound at her mistress' distress. The speckled cat proceeded to rub her face against Naomi's chin.

The witch reached up to pet the cat absentmindedly. "That's a problem. A huge one. That means they're not leaving here until they break my wards. You're too valuable to give up, and now they know it."

She swore again and I took half a step back. I hadn't even heard some of the words coming out of her mouth before.

She spun and called to the fairies. "Conference!" she yelled.

"Conference?" Fianna called back. "Are you out of your damn mind? We're in the middle of a freaking battle. There's no time for a conference. If we don't keep reinforcing these wards of yours, they're getting in!"

"Make time. You need to hear this."

Fianna the Crimson cursed up a tinkly storm, using some of the new words I'd heard from Naomi. "Come on. Let's go," she told Nessa with an exaggerated scowl, and the two fairies flew toward our position next to an interior partition wall, as far away from the exterior windows as we could get.

The moment they were next to us, Fianna said, "Well? If we don't fight back, this house is coming down with us in it. You've got thirty seconds."

Naomi said, "The girl revealed her true nature to a vamp, and the witch they have with them is as strong as I am."

"Dammit!" Fianna swore. "We have to get out of here. They'll never give up now."

"Precisely."

"Can you do it?"

"Yes, as long as I can count on you to distract

them, the witch especially. If she catches on to what I'm doing and blocks me, we're done for."

"Do you know who it is?" Nessa asked.

"I've narrowed it down to three possibilities, and all three options are bad."

"All right," Fianna said. "Where are we going?"

"Wait," I said. "Going? What about Quinn and Irving?"

Nessa looked at me with wide, sympathetic eyes, and I had my answer. "No," I protested. "We can't leave them behind. I'm *not* leaving them behind. I can't."

"You have to," Nessa said. "We have no other choice now."

"And what if they're out there getting hurt right this instant?"

The blue fairy flew over to me and placed a hand on my bare arm. It was so small I barely felt her touch. "Irving has a reputation for being fierce. The other shifters are scared of him."

"Irving? Really?"

The fairies nodded, so I looked to Naomi. "It's true," she said. "The other shifters won't mess with him unless they have to."

"But what if they find out—?"

"Shhh," Fianna snapped. "Don't mention anything—or *anyone*—else." Her meaning was pointed and clear. "Vamps hear everything."

"Even this plan," Nessa grumped.

The house shook again as if we were in the epicenter of a violent earthquake. Plaster rained down on all of us, coating each of us in white dust. I coughed so hard my esophagus hurt.

"Where do we go?" Naomi mouthed, Petunia still perched on her shoulder and pressed against the side of her head. The cat's nails clamped into the witch's shoulder so hard I was sure she must be hurting under the thin layer of her dress.

"I'm not leaving," I tried again.

"Shh," Fianna snapped, and flew over to land on my ear. She bent down and whispered as the house shook us again as if it were a giant whale and us no more than barnacles upon it. "Do *not* say another word. You'll ruin it all."

That smarted, but she was right. Still, how could I leave Quinn behind? I couldn't, not when he'd protected me, not when I longed to feel close to him again and we'd only been apart for minutes. Not when I didn't know if I'd ever see him again if I left…

"We have the experience and magic that you don't," Fianna continued. "Trust us."

I didn't want to trust them; they'd been little more than terrifying since I'd met the lot of them. But what choice did I have, really? Unless I planned to run outside on my own and probably get caught in the process, there was nothing I could do to save Quinn from anything. And the hunters outside were hurling nonstop fury at the house's wards. We wouldn't be safe for long in here, especially if they kept going until they reached me.

"He'd want you safe," Fianna said in little more than a breath.

She was right, of course. Though it made no logical sense, Quinn wanted me safe. I nodded, unconcerned by the tears already welling in my eyes.

Fianna flew around to look at my face. Satisfied by whatever she saw there, she flew back to the others.

"There's only one place to go," Nessa said, but I had to stare at her lips to be sure. I scooted closer.

"Where?" Naomi mouthed.

"The Menagerie," Nessa mimed. When I arched my eyebrows in silent question, she added, "Also known as the Magical Creatures Academy." Or at least that's what I thought she said based on my lip reading.

Naomi's mauve lips pressed into a deep frown. She ran a hand along Petunia's back while she debated. When the house shook so hard that it sent me tumbling to the ground, and Naomi had to brace herself against a wall, she finally nodded.

"Do your bit," she told the fairies, "and I'll do mine."

Apparently, I no longer had a job other than to not make things any worse than I already had.

I stuck next to Naomi like a sticky sea slug and waited, unable to help that every one of my thoughts ended up with Quinn. He had to be all right. I needed to see him again. I needed to feel his touch and his eyes upon me once more.

Step one: Get out of this place before it finished falling down around us, and the vamps and the witch, and probably shifters too, swarmed in to scrape our bodies from the floor before stealing our magic from us—however power-hungry creatures went about doing that.

Naomi faced away from me when her body and Petunia's flared in a blaze of thick, viscous green magic. I realized belatedly that she wasn't aware I stood so close to her.

Her magic swept me up in it.

✴ 15 ✴

THE SHAKING, CRUMBLING HOUSE VANISHED IN AN instant, and I blinked stupidly at the all-encompassing green fog that replaced it. Naomi and Petunia, who'd been right next to me, popped up amid the green so far away from me that I had to squint to see them.

My body seemed to spin in place, forcing me to fight the urge to vomit. What was this madness? And how on earth was I in the middle of it?

I searched for the fairies but didn't spot them, though I could hear their signature tinkling that reminded me of tiny seashells chiming against each other. I lost sight of Naomi and Petunia as well and worried whatever was happening would end with me going mad. I searched for a point of stillness and came up empty. Everything that wasn't supposed to move did, taking me right along with it.

Just when I believed I couldn't stand a moment more, the surface beneath my feet, no longer any kind of floor I recognized, vanished, and I plummeted. My already knotted stomach launched itself into my throat. I opened my mouth to scream, but was too terrified to manage even that. This was worse than the vamp licking his lips like I was lunch. This was the worst thing I'd ever experienced.

I swung my arms wildly, working to do something, anything, to halt the momentum of my downward trajectory. The world continued to spin as I fell so fast that my waist-long hair traced a vertical line above my body. As if by instinct, I clamped my wings against my back so they wouldn't tear.

Wait. My wings!

They could stop my fall, assuming I wouldn't end up ripping them flush from my back. At the speed I was falling, it was entirely possible.

I shut my eyes in an attempt to close out the dizzying sights, then tilted my body so that it was horizontal to the fall—at least, I believed I was now horizontal, even that was impossible to tell. But with my body pointed in this direction, the air cut against a greater surface area, and my fall slowed, barely at all, but enough for a burst of hope.

Gradually, I lifted my wings. With my body to block the bulk of the air current rushing at me, I rose my wings painfully slowly, an inch at a time. Better to take it slow than too fast and have them shorn from my body. At this rate, the fall seemed as if it would never end anyway. Everything felt the same as when the fall had begun, and there was no end in sight anywhere.

I stretched my arms out to either side of me. Any

additional resistance I could provide via my body would protect my wings.

The long violet strands of my hair whipped and tangled in the tops of my wings, but I pushed them open some more. They did nothing to slow my fall, but they were still attached to my back, so it was progress.

My eyes and nose watered as the air rushed past me at startling speed. My ears ached, and I pushed my wings open a little more. I was alone. There were no tinkling seashell sounds or meows or anything at all beyond the air and my thudding heart, threatening to liquefy in my chest or maybe explode or some other awful thing. No body, no matter what its nature, could possibly endure this for much longer. I sensed that my time was running out. Before I could talk myself out of it, I pushed my wings out in a burst.

They caught and tugged painfully at the point where they met my shoulder blades. I cried out and whimpered, then immediately forced myself to focus on controlling my flight.

My wings had caught me. I jerked to what felt like near stillness after my plummet, and now drifted downward without control.

I opened my eyes, noticed that the swirling green around me had subsided so as to be little more than a suggestion, and got to making my wings work for me.

There was no need to pump them. I glided downward, jerkily at first, then more or less smoothly. I could finally breathe properly again, and took big inhales that served to calm my thundering heartbeat.

I could do this. Heck, I already was.

The more I drifted, the smoother my flight became. Until it almost became enjoyable—almost, because there was nothing I wanted more than to get out of this bizarro world, get in the ocean, and go home, where I assumed I'd lose my wings and could work to put the events of the day behind me.

Except for Quinn. I didn't want to forget him. I wasn't even sure I could if I wanted to. But was this odd connection between the two of us important enough to endure all I'd been through?

Yes, it was. I knew it already. Whatever Quinn and I shared, he and I had to survive to figure it out.

I was finished with this crazy business. It was time to get back to Quinn.

Just as I thought it, a wave of green skimmed across my skin before flashing so brightly I had to close my eyes to it.

Then I was falling again before I managed to catch myself with my wings. I snapped a frantic look below. Finally! A tapestry of color spread far beneath me. There was an end to this…

As I neared the earth and it crystallized into focus, Naomi and Petunia fell past me. They were plummeting, just as I'd been, their screams and screeches distorted by the speed of their fall.

Fianna, in a dive, passed me, then opened her wings to pull up next to me. Her mouth moved, and I was sure she was saying something. I just couldn't make out what.

Nessa wove between my wings and pulled up on my other side. She too appeared to be shouting at me.

I pointed to the ground beneath us. Whatever it was, surely it could wait until we landed. We were almost there. A few more hundred feet of a drop I supposed, though it was hard to gauge distance like this.

A terrified shriek had me jerking my head toward the ground, searching for Naomi and her cat. Naomi was a witch. Surely she'd brace their fall, wouldn't she?

I made out a speck of mauve and browns before Fianna tugged on my ear. I whipped my head around, shaking her loose, and scowled. What was with them? Jeez.

Where were they when I'd been falling to my death? Nowhere useful. And now that I had it under control, they wanted to bug me?

I pointed to the ground beneath us with impor- tance and steadfastly ignored the fairies' protests. They could deal. I needed to get solid ground under me immediately. There was only so much a half-siren, half-angel girl could take, and I'd passed my limit almost at the start.

Tears leaked in streams against my cheeks, but at least the air stung less now. I bit at my lip as Naomi and Petunia neared the ground and I saw no flashes of the witch's magic.

I debated whether I should go into a dive to try to save them. I didn't know how to control my wings well enough yet. I'd probably end up killing myself, and there wasn't time anyway.

The fairies! Fianna and Nessa at least could do magic. I looked to them, but their attention was on the witch and her cat below us. Like me, they waited.

At the last possible moment, green flashed around Naomi and Petunia in a cloud.

An inhale trembled through me. There hadn't been a moment to spare.

I drifted downward. Now that the world was not confined to the width of the green swirling whirlpool of Naomi's magic, I spread my wings to their fullest. I rode the wind like a bird. I banked this way and that, exploring, and despite the horrific moments of before, I smiled. *This* was something I'd never anticipated.

I was a creature both of the water and the sky, and for the first time since discovering it I suspected I might learn to enjoy it … just as soon as I figured out how to survive it.

As the ground drew close, I prepared to pull my wings in at the last moment for a graceful landing. Yeah, it didn't turn out that graceful. I barely managed to tuck my wings in before I tumbled, tripped over the feet I wasn't used to having, and thrust my hands out to catch my fall before sprawling face-first on grass.

I lay on the grass for several long breaths, relishing the feel of its stillness. The ground wasn't swirling or rushing past me in a blur; it was pure heaven. I couldn't help but smile. I'd survived. I hadn't torn my wings or vomited all over myself. Those were big wins.

I took in the beautiful, untouched landscape before me. When I went to stand, my legs wobbled and wouldn't hold my weight. I rushed back down to my knees, and when the world spun again—just once, thank goodness—I sat back down—hard.

All right, so I'd need a few minutes. That was okay. It made sense that my body needed time to recover from whatever had just happened. And what did happen?

I turned, looking for the others, and found them all staring at me, even the cat. No, it wasn't a stare; it was most definitely a glare. Not a single one of them seemed happy with me.

Naomi's hair was a gnarled whip of tangles. The fairies and the witch were filthy, as I was sure I must be; the cat's hair stood on end, pointing in a variety of directions.

Naomi fumed. Unconsciously, I pulled back, wrapping my arms around my knees and spreading my wings along my back. The witch's murderous eyes bulged in their sockets, giving off a maniacal air. She pointed a shaky finger at me, huffed, pulled it back, brought both hands to her hips, and stomped in place.

She stalked right up to me; Petunia mirrored her movements. The fairies flew over. I suspected they were worried Naomi would kill me before they could complete their mission of delivering me to the Magical Creatures Academy.

I looked around. The open field didn't look like a school, but what did I know?

"Don't you dare look away from me," Naomi seethed.

I snapped my head back. "You have no right to speak to me like that. You nearly killed me with your magic. I deserve some time to compose myself so I can actually walk." Whoa, this was good. I was actually standing up for myself for once. "I've done nothing wrong."

"You've done everything wrong," Naomi growled, and I searched for elongating teeth or claws. She sounded like an animal. "*You* are the one who almost killed us. You're the one who dropped us in the middle of nowhere instead of where I was taking us. You're the one who messed with *my* magic, so don't give me that bullshit!"

I opened my mouth to defend myself, came up short, and looked away toward the calm of the field, with its swaying grasses and crisp, happy sky above it. The sky, though bright, lacked a visible sun to illuminate it. If what she said was true, then something had gone very wrong, and as usual I had no idea what.

❧ 16 ❧

I STOOD ON SHAKY LEGS AND FACED THE ENRAGED witch and cat, and the barely less furious fairies. "All right," I said with all the reluctance I experienced at facing yet another unexplained aspect of myself. "What is it exactly that you believe I did?"

"I don't believe you did anything," Naomi said. "I *know* what you did."

"All right, then. Enlighten me!" It wasn't like I'd intended to do whatever it was they thought I'd done.

"You stole my magic."

"I did no such thing."

"You must've."

"Well, then you'd better reassess your theories, because I didn't steal your magic. I haven't stolen a single thing in my entire life."

From the surprised expressions on all their faces, even the cat's, I was the only who could make that claim.

"You have to have stolen my magic," Naomi hissed. "It's the only explanation for what happened."

"It can't be, because I didn't. So come up with another theory or this conversation is over." It was a comical threat, really, because where would I go to avoid it?

"I spun my magic to transport us all, as I've done a million times, but it didn't go the way it should've. We're supposed to be at the school, not out in the boonies." The witch waved her arms about in the air with a crazed gleam to her eyes. "Does this look like the Magical Creatures Academy to you? Huh? Does it?" she screeched.

Something in me snapped. "How the hell should I know? I've never even heard of this Magical Creatures Academy or Menagerie or whatever place until today! And lest you forget, today also happens to be the day I lost my tail, only to be replaced by these cumbersome limbs. And oh, I almost forgot, I sprouted wings and found out a whole horde of scary supernaturals are out to kill me or worse! But oh, you got me. I've been plotting and planning this for my entire lifetime. I set out to *steal* your magic and then nearly fall to my death in the process."

I crossed my arms across my chest and met their glares with just as much fire of my own. Strangely, Naomi relaxed a bit at that.

"So you didn't steal my magic…" she said.

I scowled at her, unwilling to give her anything more.

"She might have unintentionally stolen it," Nessa

said from where she hovered at eye level. When I shot her a full dose of my frustration, her voice squeaked. "Or maybe it's something else."

"Of course it is!" My nostrils flared and I pointed my nose up in the air to scent for the ocean. If I caught even a whiff of the home I left behind, I'd head back toward it. This was getting ridiculous. No one should expect me to endure all this, not even Mulunu with her wild, milky eyes.

Nessa bit at her diminutive lip and hemmed and hawed until Fianna snapped at her. "If you have something to say, say it already."

"Whoa, don't go biting my head off or I won't tell you what I just figured out."

"Fine."

"An apology wouldn't kill you either," Nessa muttered, but didn't bother waiting for one. "Okay, so. We don't know what kind of powers Selene might have, right?"

"Right," Fianna ground out.

"And we already saw that her powers reacted to Naomi's when she was setting up the wards. Of course, Quinn was there too at the time, and there's something going on there, but we'll deal with that later."

"We'd better," I said.

Nessa the Sapphire nodded distractedly. "I think all that must've happened is Selene's unactivated powers reacted to Naomi's transportation magic, and voilà!"

"Voilà what, you annoying, tinkling thing?" Naomi said.

"Watch yourself," Fianna said, and I rolled my eyes. In all my life I'd never heard so much fighting.

Nessa huffed, slapped a hand to her hip, and addressed Naomi. "What I'm saying is that she didn't steal your powers. She didn't do anything on purpose. Her magic surged in reaction to yours, probably some kind of self-defense mechanism or something, probably already on alert since your wards tried to kill her."

Naomi was shaking her head. "That makes sense, but it's got to be more than that. She didn't just take my magic or react to it, she *changed* it. She used it, and no one should be able to use a witch's magic. Every single witch in history has a special signature to her magic. The same for wizards. No one is able to use another's magic."

"Surely witches usurp others' powers all the time," Fianna said.

"Nullify, sure. Interfere with, yes. Take it to bolster their own magic, if they're powerful enough. But never actually use another witch's magic without bringing it under the umbrella of their own."

"Okay, so maybe Selene did that," Fianna said.

Again, Naomi shook her head as Petunia leapt into her waiting arms. The witch petted her cat without looking at her. "She didn't. I'd recognize the signature of my own magic anywhere. My magic was rolling off of her. She used my power to send us tumbling down that rabbit hole, the one that almost killed all of us."

"Not us," Fianna said with a smile. "We just flew through it the whole way."

"Speak for yourself," Nessa said. "I thought it was pretty brutal."

"Selene is the one who deposited us here," Naomi said. "Wherever we are." She trailed off and the fairies followed her example as she looked around.

"Yeah, where are we?" Nessa asked. "I can usually get a sense for every place..."

"*You* don't know where we are?" Fianna asked, the sudden alarm in her voice setting my heart to racing again.

Nessa spun in every direction, flying to look everywhere, white plaster dust flying loose of her azure hair, her eyes wide with fear. "I don't know where we are. That's never happened before."

"Surely we're just lost," I said, but my voice lacked confidence. The fairies, who hadn't seemed overly terrified when we were dropping from the sky, were frightened now.

"What?" Naomi asked, ignoring my hopeful suggestion entirely.

Fianna's usually lively features were drawn. "Nessa never gets lost because she always knows where she is."

"Okay, so it's a new place," I said. "So what? Everything's new about this for me."

"You don't understand. Nessa can identify every single place on the Earth. Every. Single. One."

I gulped. I was beginning to understand. "Even in the water?" That was just my merperson curiosity. We felt so disconnected from life upon land. I wouldn't like the thought of a fairy sensing my home.

"Not the water," Fianna said, "and before you ask, not the air either. All the land. Every point on Earth." The crimson fairy paused long enough to share a somber look with all of us. "If Nessa doesn't know where we are, that means we're somewhere not upon this Earth."

"No! That's not possible," I said right away. I chortled. "You can't actually be suggesting that this"—I stomped a foot on the earth, nearly losing my balance in the process; legs were tricky business—"isn't the Earth. It clearly is. It looks exactly like the Earth."

"Yeah, well, this is one of Nessa's powers. She can pinpoint her location anywhere in the world."

"Oh my goodness," Naomi gasped. She brought the hand that'd been petting Petunia up to her mouth.

"You can't be serious," I said. "I didn't steal magic, and I didn't deposit us someplace that isn't on Earth. It's not possible."

"Oh," Naomi said, "the more you discover of the powers of supernatural creatures, the more you'll discover that the most unlikely of things are possible."

"I imagine that'll be the case, but not this."

The fairies nodded at me in unison, with matching bewildered expressions.

I threw my hands in the air. "If we're not on Earth, where do you suggest we are?"

"I have no idea," Nessa said. "I don't feel the Earth."

Fianna gasped. "The Earth always sings to you."

Nessa nodded morosely. "Up until now."

"Oh, this is so not good."

"You can say that again," Nessa said. "I can't even tell in which direction we need to go to find the Earth again." The blue fairy turned toward me. "Our only hope lies with her."

I laughed. "You're joking, right?" No, they weren't. Smiles were blatantly lacking. "How can I get us back to Earth when I don't even know what I did to get us off it?—assuming I even did."

"Oh, you did," Naomi said. "That's a guarantee. My magic isn't capable of this, at least not when I'm in control of it." She bit at her lip as if she were debating whether she'd be able to replicate this result. But who would want to be so lost so as to not even be on the right planet or plane anymore? Only a crazy person, which there was a good chance Naomi might be.

"What do you expect me to do? I have absolutely no idea what to do," I said.

"Then I guess it's on us to help you figure it out," Fianna said, "because we're not getting back to where we belong until you do."

Great. Flipping fantastic.

"Hey, at least the nasties after Selene won't be able to find her anymore." Nessa smiled, and I had to appreciate the fairy's ability to find good in our situation. "That vampire is the worst of them, and he was locked on Selene."

I swallowed thickly as the image of the incredibly striking—and incredibly deadly—vampire flashed into my mind so vividly that it was like I was still standing in Irving's crumbling house, the vampire's dark eyes pinning me into place, making escape impossible. "Wh-who is he?" I asked.

Naomi smirked. "That vampire is Antonio Dimorelli. He's been around for centuries, which makes him *very* powerful." The way the witch rolled the word "powerful" revealed that she coveted more magic as much as any of those who pursued me. "More vampires die than survive. It takes one of great cunning and skill to survive this long."

Naomi paced, then turned to face me, allowing her bright eyes to trail over me as if I were a prize to be won. I gulped as she continued. "In recent years, Antonio has moved away from the rule of the clans, probably deciding it's more fun to do whatever he wants without rules."

Her eyes glimmered, and I took a step away from her. Yeah, I'd allowed myself to forget how dangerous the witch in our midst was. The greed that lit her eyes now reminded me that she chose her battles with a similar consideration as the vampire who sought to claim me. If Naomi believed she could take my power, she would—in a heartbeat. I took another step back from her, and when she noticed, a predatory flicker flashed across her icy eyes until she tucked it away.

But then Naomi gazed off into the distance. When she spoke again, her voice was dreamy, and I understood that I wasn't able to follow all she was thinking. I was too new to the supernatural community to consider every pertinent factor. "Obviously Antonio

has decided he has enough power to defy the clans …
and the Enforcers." She resumed her distracted
petting of Petunia.

"B-but he must not have that much power if he
still wants mine, right?" I squeaked, the memory of
the vampire too vivid.

Naomi stared at me, blinked dark-coated lashes,
then threw her head back in a harsh chuckle. Petunia
chuffed, and I could've sworn the cat was laughing at
me too. All mirth dropped from the witch's face.
"Child, you have no idea how much power a vampire
like Antonio Dimorelli has. He could snap you like a
twig, and he's so good at what he does that he could
do it before you realized he'd done it, and convince
you that you liked what he'd done. A vampire like
Antonio controls your free will so masterfully that you
think you're giving yourself to him. His victims *love*
him."

Her eyes were back to glittering as … admiration
filtered into her voice. Oh man, the fairies were so
right not to trust the witch.

"And now that he's aligned himself with such a
powerful witch, one nearly as powerful as I…" She
shrugged a little too happily. "Well, the only thing that
will keep you from him is a different plane."

"And the Menagerie," Nessa said in a cautioning
tone. "Sir Lancelot will be able to keep her safe."

Naomi gave a disinterested shrug as if she either
didn't believe I'd be safe at the Menagerie or she was
rooting for this vampire Antonio. If I hadn't seen the
witch fighting to keep out the vampire and whatever

troops he had to support his fight, I would've wondered if she was enamored with him.

The sooner I put distance between myself and this witch—and her idol vampire—the better.

"Well," Nessa said in what seemed like a forced happy tone, "at least here Selene doesn't have to worry about Antonio Dimorelli or whatever witches and shifters he has on his side." Nessa smiled, and the gesture reached her cerulean eyes. "Right now, right here, she's safe, and that's great." Her smile spread into one of triumph.

"That's right," Fianna said. "You always do a good job of finding the bright side of things, Nessa."

The blue fairy grinned at the compliment and shook the many bracelets along her arms to make a tinkling celebratory sound. From what I'd observed of the spunky Fianna, she was stingy with her praise of the slightly smaller fairy.

"Have y'all gone and lost your damn minds?" Naomi barked. "There's nothing good about this. We're as stuck as it gets, and we have to rely on a total numbnuts novice to get us out of here, unless you have some tricks up your fluttery sleeves you're not telling me…"

"None," Nessa said, refusing to drop her smile as if on principle. "But hey, at least we're not dead."

With standards as low as those, any news was good news. We might be lost … somewhere … but at least we were alive. All I could do now was hope Quinn and Irving were alive too, even if they were on a different plane than I was.

At the thought of Quinn, I rubbed my hands together, determined to find something useful to do. If we were relying on me to get us out of here, then we had our work cut out for us. "Where do I start?" I asked.

Not a single woman there looked like she had an inkling of an answer, but they all talked at once anyway.

❧ 17 ☙

I STARED AT MY BARE OPEN PALMS FORLORNLY. "Nothing, see. No magic. No spark. Nothing at all."

I uncrossed my legs and stretched them out in front of me on the ground, which definitely wasn't normal ground. Though on first inspection this place resembled Earth, it had revealed itself as a poor imitation. The grass was insubstantial. As if every detail were made of wisps of empty air, a play of shadows and illusions, when I ran my hands across the grass I felt nothing beyond a rush of energy. Individual blades didn't caress my skin.

No insects or worms crawled across the dirt that appeared beneath the grass. No birds circled the cloudless, impeccable sky. Even the air felt wrong the more I sucked it in, as if it were insufficient to nourish my lungs. And yet the "ground" held me as I sat upon it. The discrepancies were enough to unnerve the more experienced fairies and witch. Petunia the cat especially didn't like it here. She was jumpy, hackles raised, as she glared at our surroundings with untrusting yellow eyes.

Still, I was only one girl, and a clueless one at that. "I've been trying for hours. I need a break."

"No time for breaks," Naomi said, peering down at me imperiously with menacing eyes. "We need to get out of here before something happens."

"Before something happens? What might happen?"

"We have no idea, and that's the problem. With magic involved, a whole variety of nasty things might happen before you get us out of here."

"There isn't magic here. That's the problem. I don't have any magic."

"You—"

I cut Naomi off. I'd heard it all before. "I might have magic, but none that's responding to my commands the way you say it should. I don't feel it at all. I don't feel any magic in this place."

Nessa flew closer and landed on my knee. "There's always magic, whether you feel it or not. Magic is everywhere. Even here..." But she trailed off.

"Wait, do you not feel the magic here?" I asked.

The upbeat fairy had become much less so as my failed attempts at getting us out of here piled up. She shared a meaningful look with Fianna before finally shaking her head. Even her blue hair, as bright as the cloudless sky, was droopy. "I don't feel a thing. It makes me feel ... empty inside."

Nessa the Sapphire dissolved into sobs. She plopped down on my leg with a loud sniffle, her translucent wings flopping against her back like wet kelp. "I don't like this one bit."

"Well, what's to like?" Naomi said with her usual personal mixture of aggression and impatience, but at least she didn't call the fairy names. She'd done plenty of that since we'd arrived here too. The longer this took, the meaner she became. That alone was reason enough to get out of here. I couldn't wait to get away from Naomi.

I tried to soothe the diminutive fairy slumped on my leg, but I didn't know what to do. There seemed no safe place to touch her where I could be sure I wouldn't cause her harm. Even though I wasn't particularly large for a girl, to the hummingbird-size fairy I must be a giant. I finally placed my hand next to her on my bare thigh, above my knee, figuring at least the proximity of my touch might accomplish something.

Fianna, however, didn't seek to console the other fairy. She got right in Naomi's face instead and glared at her, buzzing her wings like an angry mosquito.

"What is it, little fairy?" Naomi asked, examining her fingernails. Petunia rubbed against her mistress' heels and the bits of leg her curve-skimming dress revealed. The cat studied the flying fairy as if she were a tasty treat.

"You need to back off, do you hear me? We've all had enough of your crap," Fianna snapped.

"Here, here," Nessa said with a pathetic sniffle.

"You have no right to make everyone else miserable. We're all stuck in the same boat right now. So shut it and deal with it."

I expected Naomi to unleash her razor sharp tongue, but surprisingly she just ran a hand through her hair and sighed. "We've been here for far too long already."

"We don't know that," Fianna said. "There's no sun here. No moon. No way to tell the passing of time."

"Precisely. Time could be passing very differently here than it is back on Earth. What seems like a minute to us might be a year."

I stared at them, my mind struggling to process that possibility. "You can't be serious," I whispered.

"Deadly," Naomi said. Of course she'd choose that word. Why would she want to bother making anything better for anyone else?

Nessa cried softly and hiccupped. The blue fairy was all but folded in on herself atop my leg. I blinked back my own tears at the thought that the Earth we finally managed to return to might be so different than the one we left behind. Quinn … he'd been my age. That couldn't change. Whatever the connection between us was, I wouldn't be responsible for changing anything about it.

He was still possibly fighting for his life and that of his uncle while we were stuck here. That vampire, Antonio Dimorelli, had been bad enough, but who knew what kind of other creatures might have awaited Quinn outside? The kind that would align themselves with a vampire like Antonio…

I licked parched lips. My skin felt dry and brittle

after so much time outside of the ocean. I needed at the least to drink water, but we had no supplies here.

I swiped the messy hair from my face, flicked the long strands back across my shoulders, where they promptly tangled with my wings, and sucked in some resilience. I wouldn't ask the witch and fairies to allow me to rest again. I'd trudge through, especially since they'd denied my request every time.

"All right. Tell me what to do."

Nessa hiccupped. Naomi and Fianna opened their mouths to speak at the same time. I held up a hand to stop them. "Not the same things you've already told me. We need a new approach. If I can't access my own powers in the way you think I need to—"

"Not think, know," Naomi interrupted.

"Whatever," I said. "How can we—I—do it if what I've tried already hasn't worked?"

No one moved to answer for once.

I added, "We need to find something different to try. What can that be?"

Fianna glanced at Nessa, then said, "The best route would be to clamp on to Nessa's magic and use it to pinpoint our destination. But she can't feel the Earth."

Nessa's chest heaved as if she'd lost a dear family member instead of a planet. A tiny sob tore from her chest.

"Aw. There, there," I said, awkwardly tracing the tip of my pinky finger along the line of her back between her drooping wings. Her breath hitched as another cry rattled through her, and she leaned into my touch.

Fianna said, "If she can't feel the Menagerie, then I truly have no idea how we'll get there."

I glared at the crimson fairy as Nessa seemed to dissolve into a puddle of grief. She sprawled onto my leg like a dying starfish, limbs sticking out to all sides as she allowed despair to flow through her. I ran my pinky finger along one of her outstretched arms, wishing there was more I could do for the distraught fae.

But Fianna was busy stroking her lips, deep in thought. "Unless…" she started. "Unless we can go somewhere else. Once we're on Earth, Nessa will be able to get us where we need to go."

"*I'll* be able to get us where we need to go," Naomi said. "I'm the one with the transport magic."

"But Nessa will be the one to guide you," Fianna said.

"I don't need—"

"Oh enough already, witch. We have bigger fish to fry than your ego."

Naomi opened her mouth, then shut it, and reached down to pick up Petunia. Once in her arms, she petted the cat in fast, furious strokes.

But she didn't say a word. Finally!

Fianna nodded her approval and flew over to land on my other thigh. She looked up at me, craning her head far back as if my face were a mountaintop. "There's another reason you really need to hurry." She grimaced and my stomach churned. Please no.

No more reasons to instill desperation in me. I was already doing the best I could.

"Our power wanes the longer we remain here," she said, and I thought my chest would burst from the pressure.

I was two seconds away from a total freak-out meltdown. From the alarmed look on Fianna's face, she knew it.

"It's okay, girl. Breathe. Just breathe," Fianna said.

I worked on breathing in the thin air that surrounded us, but Naomi paced furiously in front of me, all the while petting that cat of hers with quick, obsessive strokes.

Fianna shot Naomi a nasty look, but quickly met my eyes again. "We'll figure it out. Just breathe through it." Her voice was artificially calm, but hey, I'd still take it. I obeyed and breathed, keeping my attention pinned on the fairy. I missed my ocean home so desperately that I wouldn't allow myself to think of the feel of the water against my skin; if I did, I'd end up in a puddle of desolation alongside Nessa.

"Our powers might be waning, but perhaps yours aren't," Fianna added.

I was about to protest and explain, yet again, that I didn't have any, so they couldn't be waning or not waning, as it were, but Fianna was shaking her crimson head even as I thought it, flakes of plaster continuing to shed from her shoulder-length hair. "We don't know anything about your powers, and neither do you. There's hope, no matter what you're thinking, or how you're feeling. You're a sirangel for goodness' sake."

"She's right," Nessa snuffled while staring up at the bright empty sky, the one that should've had a sun or a moon, a cloud or a bird, something, anything, to feel more like home. "It takes time, often a long time, for a new creature to come into her—or his—powers. You're doing great."

"I-it can take a while?" I asked.

"Of course." Nessa hiccupped again.

"Well, why didn't anyone tell me that before?"

"Because we don't have time for you to dillydally," the witch said.

"Naomi…" the tiny red fairy warned, and the witch grew quiet.

Fianna continued: "For a creature like you, new to everything on land"—at the mention of Earth, Nessa whined and flung her head to the side in a dramatic gesture; Fianna rolled her eyes where the other fairy couldn't see her—"it makes sense for your magic to feel foreign, out of reach. Especially since there are no others of your kind to guide you or teach you some tricks. Nessa and I had an aunt who taught us much of what we know."

"You did?" The pressure in my chest was beginning to lighten.

Fianna nodded, red hair bouncing. "She showed us the way until we could continue the path of learning on our own. Of course it helped that Nessa loves books so much. And that I have such an astute mind and excellent observational skills. I'm also great with other creatures."

Naomi snorted, as did her cat. Fianna ignored them, trailing a ticklish circle around my thigh as she walked. "We were soon able to figure out all sorts of things without Aunt Sosie's help."

"Wow. That's really great," I said. "So does that mean you're sisters? Or cousins?"

Nessa smiled faintly and nodded, sweeping blue hair up and down her spot on my leg. "We're first cousins. Our mothers are sisters. That's why I put up with Fianna's obnoxious tendencies—"

"Hey!" Fianna protested.

Nessa looked up at the blank azure sky. "Either way, we stick together."

"I've remained quiet as long as I could," Naomi said. "But you surely can't think this is the time for family history. My power is slipping away from me!"

Fianna didn't even look at the witch, only back at me. She held my eyes and narrowed her features into determined lines. "You've got this. You just need to fast-track some of your learning is all. You for sure have powers, no doubt about it."

When the panic erupted across my face again, she shook her head. "It's okay, really. The magic you come up with doesn't need to be fancy or perfect. We just need to ride it back to Earth. Anywhere on Earth will do. Nessa can guide us the rest of the way." As if she feared another of the witch's interruptions, she quickly added, "And Naomi can transport us there."

I focused on deepening my breath, doing my best

to ignore how thin the air tasted, doing what I could to prepare myself for pushing through to success. "So it doesn't have to be great … just get us there…"

"That's right. It's simpler than what you fear. There's no way, at all, that the first daughter of a siren and an angel won't have at least some of their magic."

I nodded, wanting her to convince me. Her pep talk had to work, because I had to do this.

"And why do you think my powers wouldn't be weakening if all of yours are?" I asked.

"It's a guess, but an educated one," Fianna said. She stopped moving across my leg to peer up at me, fists clenched to either side of her. She was going to pep talk the current out of me, all right. "Selene, your parents are from the sky and the sea. Though I realize the ocean is part of the Earth, and that the same Earth that we fairies are connected to runs beneath it, the water has a different feel to it. A different magic all its own."

"Absolutely," I said. "The ocean feels very different from land."

"Exactly. Which means that of all of us here, you're the one most likely not to lose her powers when we're away from the Earth. We fairies rely on the earth for our magic. It's the source of all our power. The earth lends us her magic so we can take care of her and her creatures."

Fianna smiled tenderly at Nessa, who'd stopped crying and was rubbing at her eyes with diminutive fists. When Nessa looked Fianna's way, the crimson fairy dropped the smile before Nessa could spot it, returning to kickass fairy in a snap. She tucked her hands behind her back and said, "All fae are connected to the earth, but Nessa has a special connection to it, one I don't have. Maybe there's still a way to merge with her connection and get us back to Earth."

I nodded, trying to believe that it'd be easy.

Nessa sat up, sprawling her hands behind her while staring up at me. I craned my neck lower so I wouldn't seem like such a giant to the fairies. "Your powers aren't tied to the earth as much as ours, but more to the sky and the water," the sapphire fairy said.

"There's no water here." I swallowed around a parched throat and licked at nearly cracking lips. In the ocean, I'd never once been thirsty.

"No, not that we've seen. But there's plenty of sky," Nessa said, attempting to imbue her voice with an upbeat tone that contradicted the droop to her wings.

It was as weak an argument as it got, and the fairies were well aware of the fact. Fianna worked to conceal her doubt from me, contorting her miniature crimson lips into a forced smile that came off more like a grimace. When she realized I knew it, she sighed. "Look, Naomi is a natural witch, which means she derives all her power and ability to do spell work from the earth too. We all feel our power weakening the longer we remain here. You don't."

"Yessss, but that's only because I don't feel my power at all."

"But you also still don't feel it weakening, and that's all we've got."

My shoulders slumped. Fianna flew straight toward my head like a projectile. In a flash, she was hovering so close in front of my face that I had to pull back to focus on the blur of her.

She pointed a tiny finger at me. "You are no regular supernatural creature. Get that through your thick head already, will you? *Angel* plus *siren*. That's a big friggin' deal. Angels are so powerful that we don't even know what they're capable of because they're too big and mighty to come down to Earth. Sirens are the most powerful of the merpeople. You're a cocktail of awesome and amazing. So buck up, step up, and get to it already. Because time's a wastin', and we can't afford any more of that."

She pressed her finger against my nose, squashing it. "You hear me, girl?" Her tawny eyes blazed as if lit from behind. "You can do this." She pushed against my nose and I closed my eyes. She was one big blur, and the air from her flitting wings was making my already dry eyes feel like they were about to break and crumble.

If the fairies believed in me, or at least were willing to pretend they did, I'd do it. I'd do whatever I had to do, because, well, there was no other choice.

"Back away from my face please," I said. "I'm ready."

Fianna hooted and hollered and flew back down to my thigh. "That's the way. We have places to be and people to see. Lead us out of here, sirangel."

❧ 18 ❧

I DIDN'T BOTHER TO THINK THINGS THROUGH OVERLY much. Since I had little idea what I was doing anyway, there seemed little point to it. I did, however, make sure the witch wouldn't try to kill me if I accidentally used her power again. Since I didn't know how I'd done it in the first place, I couldn't figure out a way to prevent it.

"I realize you say your powers are waning," I started, "but—"

Naomi cut me off. "If you find yourself drawing on them, that's fine—in this one and only instance, you understand me."

"I totally do. It won't ever happen again— assuming it happens this time."

The witch stood directly in front of me, though she hadn't ceased petting Petunia. The cat didn't protest, however. There was an odd connection between the witch and her pet. She said, "Do whatever you need to do to get us out of here. But by the love of all things holy and unholy, get us the hell out of here."

I nodded. "Right. I'm on it." At another time I would have laughed at my empty assurances. Now I wouldn't dare. I was the only shot we had. I purposely hadn't asked what would happen if I didn't lead us away from here. I ran my hands across the "grass" beside me, and when an empty sensation like a cool breeze was all that met my palms, my heart thumped with urgency. Despite its idyllic appearance, this place was unnatural. This plane, wherever it was, wasn't equipped to sustain life.

"Take flight," I said to the fairies still on my legs. They responded right away, but remained close by as I stood awkwardly, still trying to get a handle on moving on two appendages with gigantic wings attached to my frame.

I closed my eyes to focus, then popped them back open. "Wait a minute. Are we going to go through what we did when we came here? Because I'm not sure I can survive another journey like that one."

"No one wants another journey like that one," Naomi said. "Do your best to avoid it, but in the end, what's most important is to get us back to a dimension we recognize."

Sure, okay. Piece of kelp pie.

I swallowed my nerves around a scratchy throat and closed my eyes again. At least that way I looked as if I had a clue, and pretending was the first step to doing magic, right? It seemed like it should be.

I could at least go through the motions. I'd seen

Mulunu connect to her sea crystal and the magic it channeled through her staff enough times. I'd do what she did.

I spread my arms out to the sides as I'd seen her do hundreds of times. Palms pointing upward toward the cloudless, sunless sky, I waited for the magic.

I wasn't sure what Mulunu felt when it first touched her. The sea witch was nothing if not reserved with her secrets. But I had a vivid imagination.

I tilted my face up toward the nonexistent sun and pulled in deep inhales, envisioning the air as rich and alive as it was on Earth, not this thin, artificial-feeling substance.

I focused on the way my torso rose and fell with my breath, with the way the air fueled my life. Therein must be magic. Air gave life. That was as close to magic as anything else.

I longed for whatever guidance the fairies and witch might offer, but we'd tried that and it hadn't worked. My own ideas were all I could count on now.

I rooted my feet to the ground, working to override the image of my tail, the one I missed as if it had been hacked off instead of transformed. I pretended my bare soles sank into the grass heavily, and I imagined the dirt of Earth beneath my feet—there, I even smelled it … the rich, nearly pungent smell of the humus of the forest behind Irving's house.

My heart fluttered toward Quinn and whatever sparked between us, but I staunchly moved it along to the here and now; I needed to find a way to survive.

I opened my wings to their fullest. As the air rushed through their feathers, I pulled on that richness —whether imagined or real, I didn't know anymore.

I imagined the sun warming my face, my bare shoulders, my stomach, and legs, the air nurturing all aspects of my living organism. I even called on the memories of the surf crashing upon craggy rocks and spraying my face with mist. I *felt* the water.

Then, without conscious decision, I envisioned myself pulling on Fianna's magic. Once I experienced a warm tingling in my center, I reached for Nessa's. With the powers of both fairies within me, tingling warmth swept all the way across my body and down my limbs, awakening my fingers and toes. I even felt it through my wings, which I hadn't truly felt before, I realized.

I registered tiny gasps, but they remained apart from the space I held myself in. I was somewhere separate, as if lulled by the ocean's soothing rhythm, delivering me to a place within myself I didn't share with anyone.

The witch was next, though in this space I felt her free from her attitude. I sensed green energy sparking and jumping to meet me. It was easy to reach out an invisible hand and latch onto it, pulling it toward me.

I was surprised when the cat's energy leapt to join Naomi's. I'd forgotten about the cat here, in this hazy, hypnotic space I occupied. But the cat's power, green and identical to Naomi's, was with me now. Somehow a part of me.

"It's not possible," Naomi, who'd said nothing was impossible, whispered somewhere far away.

I thought of the singing birds I loved to listen to on Earth, when they perched on rocks in the sea especially, squawking raucously. I pictured the scents of the forest where Quinn might be, and breathed in the scents of green life and rich dirt, as I imagined he might be right then too.

A blue energy throbbed and called for my attention. As if in a drugged stupor, I dragged myself toward it. Its bright light pulsed, dimming then brightening all over again.

It called to me as poignantly as a siren's song.

So I followed it. I wasn't sure whether my legs were moving or whether my wings were, or whether anything moved at all. I followed the pinging blue light the best way that I could—with all my heart.

This blue energy was pleasant, warm and breezy like the perfect sunshiny day. I glided with it, following the course it laid out for me. Every time I thought I was about to reach it, the blue blinking light moved away. I followed. It moved more, and I followed again.

I had no idea how long this went on, but I didn't want it to end. I was happy here, wherever I was. My exhaustion was absent, my thirst and hunger gone. I was content, wrapped in the calm of Mother Earth, in the seas that had sung to me since I was an infant. Her lullaby would always bring me home.

I moved effortlessly, always toward that light that beckoned.

Until it finally stopped moving. I embraced the blue light, inviting it inside me, joining with it as one.

"Ah," I sighed. *This* was home. This was peace and contentment. There was nowhere else I needed to go.

"Selene! Wake up!" a tinny voice called.

I ignored it.

"Selene," called another voice, and I grumbled mentally, *Leave me alone*.

Then someone shook me. I pulled back, resisting the disruption to the calm within.

The shaking only became more insistent, as if I were back in that crumbling house with its vicious predators. A shake so powerful my head rattled. "Hmm. No," I complained, this time out loud, though I couldn't be certain. There was no one else here with me in my center, so it shouldn't matter anyway. And I should be able to resist the disruptions. They were in my imagination alone, and I could override them. My fears had no place here, none at all.

"No! Don't go back in. Don't push me away."

The voices grew fainter and I smiled my triumph. Yes, back to the calm so like the soothing, lulling ocean that gentled my heart.

"Sirangel girl, dammit, wake up before you tug us back to that blasted wasteland," a harsh voice commanded.

"She's taking us back!" a desperate voice called. It was no longer directed at me.

"We have to stop her if she won't wake up," said a voice, small in volume only.

"My magic is back. I'll stop her." The wicked voice seemed possibly pleased at the prospect.

Then my ears and nose were yanked, hard, jerking me from my space of well-being. I popped open my eyes before I could halt the self-preservation reaction.

A blur of red and blue tugged on my upper eyelashes and refused to let me shut my eyelids again. The blue fairy flew in front of my gaze, a blur I struggled to bring into focus.

"Selene, you did it. You brought us here. But you can't go away again. Stay here. Keep us here, *please*." Sapphire eyes welled with tears. "The earth is singing to me again. Please don't make me lose that. I don't think I could bear to lose her another time."

The depth of emotion in her plea led me to concentrate on the blue fairy.

"That's it," she said. "That's it, Selene! Keep going. Stay focused on me. You're almost back." She clapped her hands giddily and grinned so wide that the smile lit her entire face.

I recognized that joy as the blue energy I'd followed to this place. I latched onto it again, this time in the form of an ecstatic, dancing fairy.

"Is she back?" sounded above my eye.

The witch swam into focus behind the blue fairy. I wasn't drawn to her energy, but the scowl she wore was sufficient to remind me that I wasn't in a peaceful place. In fact, she represented all the danger I had to ward against.

Quinn. I thought of the hybrid shapeshifter I barely knew but who called to me as fiercely as the ocean. He was the final piece of the puzzle. I had to find my way to him.

"I'm back. I'm here," I said, before I fully was. "Drop my eyelids."

The fairies released me and I moved to take in my surroundings for the first time. They were nothing like what I'd imagined.

❧ 19 ❧

"WHERE ARE WE?" I ASKED. WHILE THE FOREST THAT surrounded us was pleasant and a welcome reprieve from, well, wherever we'd been, it wasn't the woods behind Irving's house. The trees here were wide and so tall that I had to tilt my head back to find their tops. It was magical, but I had the feeling we were still far from Quinn and the danger we'd left him in.

"We're home," Nessa squealed, whirling in the air. "We're on Earth, and my magic is back at full strength. It's a happy day." She turned in flight again, but this time azure sparkles ran the length of her small body, resulting in a change of attire. Restored were her blue skirt and tiny top, complete with the ruffles that adorned their edges. She breathed in through her grin. "Doesn't it feel glorious?"

Fianna matched her grin for a quick moment, but I suspected it was as much because she was pleased to see the teary-eyed fairy back to her usual self as to celebrate our return to Earth. Fianna flew over to me, her eyes alight but her expression serious. "How'd you do it?" she asked while flying in my line of sight.

Naomi appeared behind her. Did the witch ever smile? Even her cat seemed to be peering at me with a heavy amount of scrutiny.

I ignored the witch and cat and focused on the crimson fairy. "I wish I had a good answer for you, but the truth is that I don't know."

"Of course you know," Naomi snapped. "No one can do that kind of magic without a clue. The fact that you think we'll believe you is preposterous." She flicked a hand in the air as if physically dismissing my claims.

"I don't really care what you think," I replied, and was shocked to discover I really meant it. "I don't know what I did. I just"—I shrugged—"envisioned myself happy, I guess."

Naomi scoffed violently. "That's ludicrous. You imagined yourself 'happy'? Give me a break. How stupid do you think we are?"

I didn't particularly think her stupid, but I was tempted to say it just to spite her.

Fianna snapped, "Apparently *you*'re pretty stupid if you won't back off and let her tell us."

"Tell us what? You heard her. She felt *happy*." Naomi's face contorted at her mocking tone, and my jaw automatically tightened at her mimicry.

"Ignore her," Fianna told me. "And that mean cat of hers too."

The cat hissed behind the fairy and jumped at her,

paws outstretched, claws extended. The fairy easily zoomed out of reach with a mocking tinkly laugh.

"Are you sure it's wise to mess with her?" I asked.

"Don't you worry about that pussycat. She's all fluff."

Yeah, I was pretty sure Fianna was dead wrong about that.

"Let's get back to the important stuff," Fianna said. "Surely there's a bit more to how you brought us here than feeling happy."

"There must be, I suppose, but I'm not sure what I did. I followed a blue blinking light here, though." I smiled at Nessa.

She beamed back at me. "That was smart of you, using my magic to help guide you. I knew you could do it."

"Well, thanks for letting me."

Hacking sounds drew my attention back to Naomi. She was pretending to be gagging. "Will you cut the love-fest already? In case you haven't realized, tinkle brains, we're in the middle of the Magical Creatures Academy, and that's not good."

"What do you mean?" Nessa said. "That's great. This is where we wanted to be."

"This is where you wanted to be, but not where Irving wanted you to bring her."

"You're not one to talk," Fianna interjected. "You witches are all about skulking around doing magic when others aren't aware of it. You're sneaky."

I expected Naomi to reply in her usual caustic fashion, but she actually looked pleased with herself.

"You're only bummed," Fianna continued, "because we're not where you wanted to take her."

Naomi didn't deny it, and my stomach churned with nerves. I hadn't trusted the witch, but neither had I realized she might have been plotting against me while I fumbled along, oblivious.

"Where did you want to take her?" the crimson fairy asked, trailing suspicious eyes up and down the witch's body, down to the cat that now rubbed itself against her calves. "To your coven?" Fianna whipped her scarlet hair around in emphasis.

Naomi examined her shiny fingernails as if the fairies hadn't spoken. She took in the state of her dress, sighed heavily, and closed her eyes. In the next instant, green light surged from her body in a thick cloud. When it settled, her dress, heels, nails, and lips were deadly black.

She cackled, looking at me in the same way Petunia looked at the fairies.

I understood exactly what that look meant and I gulped. Fianna flew in front of me as if to defend me. "Don't you dare do anything to her. You hear me?"

"Or what? What will you tiny little insignificant fairies do to me if I decide to take the sirangel with me? Irving isn't here to protect you now, and you know what I'm capable of."

I hoped the fairies would put her threats to shame, but instead they shared a nervous look that set my nerves to tingling. I sat up straighter, arranging my wings behind me so their tips would bend along the ground next to me. I was sitting on real grass; the dampness of the earth beneath me chilled my legs. I should've been thrilled at the sensation after the fake grass of that other dimension. Instead, the chill settled deep inside me. What midday sunlight managed to filter through the towering trees didn't warm me. Goosebumps erupted all over my bare legs and arms. Naomi was looking at me much as the vampire Antonio Dimorelli had: like I was lunch.

Fianna said to Nessa, "You'd better go get Sir Lancelot."

Naomi threw her head back and laughed stridently. How could Irving have had any kind of dealings with someone like this? Maybe she'd concealed her true nature; she seemed capable of all kinds of deceit.

"The talking owl?" Naomi taunted. "The one who's barely larger than any of you? Fine, go fetch your precious owl. I'll be long gone with the sirangel before you return."

Fianna's little shoulders squared and she gave Nessa a look that clearly said, *Go, and fly like the wind.*

Nessa was off like a shooting star, while Fianna zipped in front of me, forming a very petite wall between me and the witch.

"You're not taking her anywhere," Fianna said, and magic crackled to life, bright crimson arcing between her facing palms.

"I'll do whatever I want with her," Naomi said, taking several predatory steps toward us. I got my act together and clambered to my feet. "Her power will be wasted here," the witch said.

"So the better option is for you to take it?" Fianna said.

"Of course."

"You're nutso, lady."

"No more than you, *fairy*."

"What would you do with her if you took her?" Fianna asked, and she actually looked … curious.

"I don't need a coven. I'd take her power for myself obviously. It's wasted on her. She doesn't even know how she returned us to Earth, or how she removed us from it in the first place. More ridiculous a thing I've never heard."

"That's only because you apparently don't register the gibberish that exits that poisonous mouth of yours," Fianna said.

"Her power is compatible with mine. She was kind enough to reveal that. It will suit me quite well." The witch turned in the direction Nessa had flown off. "Well, it's time for us to be going. That owl of yours isn't a threat, but rumors say he won't shut up. No one has time for that."

Fianna scoffed at her hypocrisy.

"Come now, sirangel," the witch said, as if I'd actually just walk right over to her and go along with her plan.

Fianna growled like an animal. "Over my dead body."

Naomi flicked her blond hair. "With pleasure."

The cat leapt into her waiting arms, and Naomi's green glow surged to encompass them both.

The fairy didn't wait for the witch to attack first.

Fianna flung her magic straight at her, red sparks aimed for her head.

The witch grunted. Petunia climbed to her shoulder. The moment both her hands were free, she flicked them in front of her. Green energy pooled in her palms and she threw arcs of menacing magic straight at the little fairy, who squealed and zoomed out of the way, already launching more red magic at the witch. She flew, bobbing and dodging as she looked over her shoulder. But Naomi was unrelenting. She pursued Fianna with her green magic, and I understood that if her magic caught the fairy unprotected, it would be the end of her. I didn't know whether it'd result in her death, but whatever happened it'd be as bad as death. It was clear from the stricken expression on Fianna's normally ferocious face.

Fianna threw bolts of red at Naomi, hitting her face, chest, and legs while flying around the tight clearing in the forest, bobbing to avoid counterattacks. And though Fianna's magic was powerful enough to break through Naomi's green magic that wrapped her like a shield, it wasn't slowing her sufficiently. Naomi winced and grunted as each stream of crimson melted the top layer of her flesh, but she persisted.

Naomi nailed Fianna with a shot of green and the fairy yelped, stumbling in mid-flight. With a cry, she pumped her wings furiously, but she was losing altitude, though her wings beat double-time.

Naomi gave chase, racing across the glade, though her heels slowed her. Fianna pulsed her wings with tiring speed and just barely managed to launch herself above the witch's head, dodging the cat's claws, while shooting red beams into her crown. The smell of burnt hair wafted through the small clearing, but Naomi didn't slow. She bit her lip in furious concentration. I realized this next blast would be the end of the fairy with enough attitude to fill someone a hundred times her size.

I didn't think, I moved. I didn't reach for whatever magic I might find. I didn't even think to connect to the witch's power to interfere, a move that might have actually worked given how I'd used her magic before. I reached a hand out to Naomi with no idea what I intended to do. Fianna shot me a look of alarm and I suspected that coming in contact with her green shield might be devastating. The fairy was careful to avoid touching it even as she drilled red sparkling light into the witch's cranium.

Fianna shook her head desperately at me, but Naomi snarled wickedly and thrust her hands up above her head to launch the killing blow to the scarlet fairy.

"No," I said and reached through the green of her magic to touch her arm.

The instant I pressed the fingers of one hand against her blistered forearm, she vanished, and the mean cat vanished with her.

❧ 20 ❧

Fianna persisted in flying as best she could though her wings had holes in them, still streaming crimson magic downward. Then bewilderment lit her face, her magic fizzled and sputtered, and she made her way over to me.

Chest heaving, she landed on my shoulder with a crash, tumbled, and plummeted toward the ground before catching herself at the last moment, more or less sticking her landing. "Oh, my wings!" she cried, but her voice was soft as it traveled the length of my body to reach me.

Despite her grave injury, Fianna didn't waste time wallowing. She caught her breath and called up to me. "Selene, what did you do?"

"I'm sorry, I don't know. I didn't mean to, I just…" I trailed off.

"No, you misunderstand me. Whatever you did, I'm so grateful you did it that you have no idea. I've just never seen anything like it before."

I stared at her, unable to decide what to think. I mean, I *really* had no clue how I'd made the witch and her cat disappear. *Poof!* They were both gone without a trace.

"You saved my life, and I'll owe you forever for that. I would have been mortified if that witch had been the end of me. It would've killed me to give someone like her the satisfaction."

I doubted Fianna was this sincere or this forthcoming often. I nodded though I wasn't sure if the fairy could see my head movements from down by my feet. "I don't, I mean, how…?"

"That's an incredibly good question. It also makes it all the more important that Naomi didn't get her greedy manicured hands on your powers. Imagine the nasty stuff she would have done with even a drop of your magic." The little fairy's voice shook at the thought.

Fianna began walking up my leg, her miniature body horizontal to my ankle and then my shin. How she remained upright, I had no idea, but her teeny bare feet tickled. "You shouldn't feel bad for what you did, Selene. You had to, truly you did."

"Oh, I know that. She was about to kill you. I just wish I understood what happened. If I can do that … whatever it is … without realizing it, am I a danger to everyone around me?"

"No, certainly not," Fianna said right away, but there was no way she could be sure. We didn't understand a single thing about my magic, which I clearly had in spades; there was no denying it anymore.

"Where did you send her, do you think?" the fairy asked. I had to work not to fidget as she crossed my knee, her injured wings tucked firmly against her back so they wouldn't hang behind her as she climbed. I shrugged, resisting the tickle as the fairy crossed onto my thigh.

"So you have no clue where you sent her?" Fianna asked.

"None at all. I didn't even mean to send her anywhere. I only meant to prevent her from hurting you."

"By reaching a hand through her magic, which should have fried you, and touching her?" Incredulity dripped from the fae's words.

I shrugged again, feeling too much like an ignoramus flung into battle. If Mother were aware of the dangers Mulunu had exposed me to, she'd kill the sea witch, or at least she'd try. Mother was gentle, graceful, and kind … until she had reason not to be. She'd always been my great protector. I missed her then so intensely that it hurt.

"Why couldn't I be normal?" I said to myself, only belatedly realizing the fairy hung on my every word.

She gasped. "Why would you ever want to be normal when you're this magnificent?"

I blinked rapidly, embarrassed that her question had moved me. No one had ever said anything like that to me before, not even Mother or Liana. When I first met the fairies, I never imagined any of them would be saying it to me now—especially not the spitfire redhead.

"You're incredible, Selene," Fianna said, continuing to climb. "Remarkable. A miracle."

My cheeks colored. "Psh. A miracle? Come on."

"Any girl that rushes in to save the fae is a miracle in my book. You've got a fairy on your side for life."

"Hmm," I said, because I wasn't entirely sure I wanted the saucy fairy in my life forever.

"There's no one more loyal than a fairy who owes a debt," Fianna said from my hip and still climbing. When she crossed onto my bare stomach, I couldn't help but twitch. "You've earned my undying loyalty. If not for you, I'd be a crisp, and what worse way to die than at the hands of that nasty-ass witch." She shuddered. "She's cuckoo. Totally off her rocker." She circled her tiny hand in the air around her ear. "Coooo-kooo." Then she smiled. "But now she's gone."

Her smile flickered as she trailed up my side. "Somewhere ... it'd be very helpful to know where."

"Why?" I asked, sure I didn't want to know the answer even before it arrived.

"Because magic and supernatural creatures are composed of energy. Energy never ceases to exist, it only transforms, or at most dissipates."

I raised an eyebrow at her.

"Which means that despicable Naomi and that nasty creature Petunia continue to exist somewhere. Because you didn't kill them, right?" Fianna was quick to add, "And know that it'd be fully all right with all of us if you did."

"I don't believe I killed them, but since I'm not sure what I actually did, or how I managed it..."

"Well, it's likely that you didn't, then. A cryin' shame." Fianna tickled along the inside of my arm as she continued her upward momentum. "Killing requires a lot of intent and a great surge of magic, at least for supernatural creatures. You probably didn't kill them if you weren't trying to. Which means they're somewhere, probably scheming and plotting already while that crazy witch clicks her ugly nails together. It'd be nice to know where they are so we can take them out before the witch tries to carry out any further attacks."

Fianna's crimson head jerked in assent of her own diatribe. "The best defense is a good offense, or at least to be aware of the movements of your enemies. And Naomi Nettles and her hideous cat are most certainly our enemies now. They just made it to the number one spot on my shit list. If I ever see them again..." She pursed her lips and shook her red head. "They'll regret ever messing with a fairy."

"I guess so," I said.

The fairy plopped down on my shoulder in a huff, breathing heavily. "Dang. I never realized what a blessing wings are. Walking ... is the worst. And you're really uphill."

Of course I was, I was standing upright. Had I thought of it, I could have offered her my hand. *You'll have to be sharper, Selene.* I'd been ten steps behind since Mulunu had waved her staff at me and I discovered myself on Irving's porch, staring into a scary wolf face.

A wolf face! Did that mean Irving was a were-wolf? Or some other wolf shifter, if such a thing existed? And what would that make Quinn if he was a hybrid as I was?

I had to find them. Just as I was about to say exactly that, Nessa appeared, flying alongside a very dignified-looking owl who might fit in the palm of my hand.

Despite his size, there was no denying he was fierce. His head swiveled in every direction, even almost entirely backward as he flew, making sure the grounds were safe, I presumed. He came in low, Nessa struggling to match his speed, and landed at my feet with enviable grace.

He peered up at me, then took in Fianna and her tattered wings. His wide yellow eyes sharpened on the fairy atop my shoulder. "What is it? What's happened?"

"Naomi Nettles nearly killed me, that's what happened," Fianna bit out. "She tore my wings before Selene here managed to get rid of her."

The owl's head tilted in my direction. "Get rid of her?" His voice was astute and intelligent, and I immediately wanted to place all my worries in his capable hands—er, wings.

When it was clear I wasn't going to explain, Fianna jumped in: "She did some kind of magic, she's not sure what. One second Naomi was closing in on me, the next, *blam*, she was gone, along with that blasted cat of hers."

"Her familiar?"

"Yes, sir."

"Familiar?" I asked in a wavering voice.

"A familiar, at least in the case of a witch of the caliber of Naomi Nettles," the distinguished owl said, "serves as a power source of sorts. Naomi draws on her cat's power to bolster her own. Almost as a battery that she recharges when she has magic to spare."

"I see. Thank you," I said.

"It's my great pleasure," the owl said, sounding like he meant it. "So you saved Fianna the Crimson by using your powers to make Naomi Nettles and her familiar disappear?"

"It would appear so."

"And where is it, exactly, that you sent them?"

"I'm sorry, but I don't know."

"Hmm, that is interesting, interesting indeed. I'll have to ponder that." He rubbed at his chin with his wing as if he were human. "Nessa tells me you're the daughter of a siren and an angel."

"That's right."

"Then you're a most unique creature."

I suspected I was no more unique than he, but I nodded anyway. "It would appear so."

"Nessa also tells me you're in need of protection."

"I believe I am."

"Then I am Sir Lancelot, headmaster of the Magical Creatures Academy, casually referred to as the Magical Menagerie, satellite school to the prestigious Magical Arts Academy. I offer you our protection, so long as we can give it."

"Thank you. I appreciate it. I'm pleased to meet you." I had to resist the urge to curtsy; that would have disastrous consequences, no doubt, since I was having enough trouble balancing on two legs. There was just something about the owl that inspired me to behave better than I usually did.

"This is the point where you're supposed to tell me your name," the owl said sternly, but when I met his eyes, I registered mirth there.

"I am Selene of the Kunu Clan, daughter of Orelia, Supreme Siren of the Kunu Clan, and Raziel of the First Celestial Order."

"That's a noble line indeed. I'm pleased to make your acquaintance, Lady Selene. Welcome to the Magical Creatures Academy, where magical and supernatural beings come to learn."

Finally. Things were starting to look up. I sure needed to learn. I smiled my thanks before Sir Lancelot opened his beak to tell me the rest of it.

After the day I had, I should have known better than to assume that things would now be easy. Simply by coming together, my parents had ensured nothing about my life would ever be easy.

🎇 21 🎇

I SOON DISCOVERED THAT NAOMI NETTLES HAD BEEN right about one thing: the owl liked to talk. I'd assumed he was ready for action given the urgency of our circumstances. Instead, it turned out that he wanted to learn every detail of the fairies' expedition since they left the Magical Creatures Academy campus. He included me in his questions at the start, but soon moved on once he realized I knew as much about what was going on as I appeared to. After that, he directed every demanding inquiry toward the fairies, who didn't seem to mind.

I'd tired of peering down at the petite creatures to follow their conversation. Finally, I sank to the grass next to them and extended my new legs. I wondered if I'd ever get used to them. Life on land was proving to be nowhere near as exotic and exciting as Liana imagined it to be. My best friend mooned over visiting land, picturing exciting adventures, fiery romances, and none of the prejudices that inhabited our clan. I wondered if I'd ever see her again and have the chance to tell her how lucky she was to be allowed to remain among the Kunu tribe.

"Thank you, fairies," Sir Lancelot was saying. "Thanks to your astute observations, I now possess a clear understanding of the situation."

The fairies beamed. Even the saucy Fianna looked pleased at the owl's compliments.

Sir Lancelot studied me with those wide yellow eyes that couldn't possibly miss a thing while he said, "It's never wise to move forward without understanding."

I didn't think he was speaking only to me, but I chortled regardless. "Then I should have remained standing outside Irving's front door and never entered his house. That wolf head knocker was certainly enough to frighten me away for good."

The owl's brow arched. "A wolf knocker?"

I waved a hand in dismissal. "It's nothing important. Just an intimidating metal wolf head on the door." I shivered at the memory of it. "It freaked me out."

Sir Lancelot turned to the fairies. "Did you see it?"

"It's not important," I said. "Let's focus on Quinn and Irving instead."

But the owl didn't reply to me, instead waiting for the fairies to respond. Fianna said, "We saw it when we staked out the place before entering."

"So you were there immediately after the wards attacked me! You weren't tired from your journey at all."

Fianna's little chin lifted. "Traveling from one place to another like that, even through a portal of my own creation, is still demanding of our energy."

"Indeed," Sir Lancelot said. "And what did you make of this knocker?"

I opened my mouth to protest since I was the one to lead them down this unproductive path, but one glance at the owl's seriousness made me shut it.

"Well," Fianna said, eyes as fierce as the owl's, "if you're thinking that head is a warning to werewolves wanting to mess with Irving and his nephew, then I'm in agreement."

"How would that be a warning?" I interjected. "Surely no shifter is as wimpy as I am."

Sir Lancelot faced me in a jerky movement and I swallowed. "A word of advice, Lady Selene of the Kunu Clan. Don't ever speak ill of yourself. There are enough in this world willing to do it for you, yet too few to think well. Be your own friend, not your enemy."

I nodded, unsure whether to feel chastened or encouraged. I was beginning to understand what the owl would want me to think.

"You weren't wimpy. Besides, Lady Selene," he continued, "from what I'm gathering, that wolf head was meant to instill fear."

"From the look of it," Fianna said, "I'd bet he succeeds in warning off those few enemies who manage to find him."

Sir Lancelot nodded, and I again realized I was

missing something. I sighed and had to ask, "What do you mean?"

"That head isn't an adornment," the owl said. "It's enchanted to appear only a knocker to those unaware of the shifter world. Perhaps if you returned and saw it now you'd see beyond the glamour."

Fianna and Nessa nodded their agreement. Nessa stroked an occasional hand in comfort across Fianna's frayed wings.

I hated to ask, but obviously I understood even less of things than they gave me credit for. "And what will I see if I look again?"

"A werewolf's head mounted on the door."

"But that's what's already there."

"He means a real head," Fianna said.

I blinked. "A real head? I'm not sure I'm following."

"Then let me spell it out for you." Fianna dropped her hands to her hips. "Irving lopped off the head of a werewolf who meant either him or Quinn harm. So other shifters would think twice before messing with either one of them, he nailed it to the door in warning. He had to have had the help of a witch to enchant it, both so it won't send the mailman running and so it won't decompose. I'm guessing Naomi effing Nettles." She pursed her blood-red lips into a thin line.

"Watch the language, Fianna. There's no call for unladylike expressions here," Sir Lancelot admonished.

Fianna looked as if she entirely disagreed, but nodded anyway. I was too busy working to wrap my mind around the fact that the little owl was perturbed not by a disembodied head but a fairy's language. What kind of world had I landed in? I gulped again, and longed for my ocean home so intensely that the sensation delivered a wave of physical pain.

Fianna climbed onto my shin and addressed the owl. "So what's the plan now?"

"Selene can remain at the school if she wishes." He made eye contact with me and I hurried to nod. My long violet hair flung all over the place in my enthusiasm to experience the safety of the Magical Creatures Academy. "I'd like that very much, thank you. But—"

"But you're concerned about this boy you have a connection with."

Quinn didn't seem much at all like a boy anymore, not with the strength that radiated from him when he aimed to protect me. "I wish to see him again, yes. And I don't think it fair that we abandoned him and Irving when those, uh, creatures were attacking. The one vampire I saw, that Antonio Dimorelli, was terrifying."

"Irving is one of the most ferocious shifters there is," Fianna said. "His reputation is well known in the supernatural community."

"And now that we've met him and Quinn," Nessa said, "we understand he endeavored to build a reputation so fierce that few would dare to bother the nephew he protects."

"Exactly. He's no pushover," Fianna agreed. "He shifts into a polar bear, for goodness' sake. There aren't many shifters who dare to take on one of the largest land creatures there is."

"A bear, you say?" I asked. "That doesn't seem right."

"Oh?" Sir Lancelot said, his voice laden with curiosity. "Why would you say that?"

"It's nothing," I replied too quickly. "I just..."

"You just what, child? You shouldn't dismiss your natural instincts. My own have saved my life more times than I can count."

"It's nothing, really," I repeated before I realized I shouldn't have. The desire not to disappoint the owl was real. I hurried to correct myself. "It's just that I sense the sea on Irving, her storms especially."

"Hm." The owl rubbed his chin with his wingtips. "That's interesting. I wonder what will come of it."

"Probably nothing at all. I don't know—"

One look from him made me press my lips shut.

"Do not deny your magic, Lady Selene. That is the quickest way to limit it."

"Okay," I said lamely, before adding, "I'd very much like to discover the extent of my magic."

The owl smiled, his cheeks rising around his beak. "Then you're in the right place."

"So does that mean I'll become a student of the Magical Creatures Academy?" Now that I was here on the campus, I wanted to stay—as long as Quinn could come too, of course. I hadn't seen the school itself yet, but maybe I wouldn't be such a freak in the midst of a bunch of magical creatures. And I'd finally get to learn!

"That isn't up to me, Lady Selene. But I dearly hope so."

The wind threatened to abandon my sails as I struggled to understand why a headmaster could do no more than hope. From what the fairies had suggested, the headmaster was in charge of the entire school. "I don't understand," I finally said.

"I don't choose," Sir Lancelot said. "No one person or creature does." An ample pause punctuated the crisp forest air. "The Menagerie chooses its own students, and it hasn't selected you yet."

Annnnnd the wind departed in a fury. My proverbial sails slumped to my sides, limp and lifeless.

22

"SURELY THE SCHOOL WILL CHOOSE HER," NESSA SAID. "She's a sirangel. Even the school will be curious."

Sir Lancelot *tsked* the blue fairy. "You know as well as I do that the school itself isn't a conscious entity. A long-lasting spell is responsible for the Menagerie's exemplary student body. It's the work of the great wizards, Lords Mordecai and Albacus of Irele, that allows the school to select the students best suited for it."

I caught Fianna rolling her eyes when she didn't think Sir Lancelot would see. I wondered whether the gesture was in reference to the owl or the students.

The owl addressed me: "I hope you'll become a part of the school, and because I do believe that will eventually become the case, I'm going to use the authority of my position to approve your stay on school grounds."

My pulse sped up.

"You won't be allowed to mingle with the students

as that would interfere with the student selection spell in place. I don't even want to think about what might happen if I attempt to introduce a student in contravention of the dictates of admission." He shivered, his beige and white feathers standing on end for a few seconds before settling back in place. "There should be no problem, however, with you remaining on the grounds."

"That's great," Fianna said. "There's no safer place than the Magical Menagerie." The owl opened his beak and the fairy hastened to add, "Other than the Magical Arts Academy, of course."

"Of course," the owl said proudly.

"So, where will she be staying?" Fianna asked.

The owl's head tilted this way and that while he considered the grounds, the fairies, and finally me. "Since you've already formed a bond with her, I think she'll stay with you."

"With us?" Fianna sputtered. "That's not fair."

I raised my eyebrows at her. This was the same fairy who said she'd owe me a life debt forever, right? Maybe "forever" was different for fairies.

"This isn't about 'fair,' Fianna the Crimson," the owl admonished.

Fianna didn't bother to look berated. "But our house is our size!" She exchanged bewildered looks with her cousin. "Where on earth do you expect us to fit her?" At the chance of perceived impertinence, she added, "It's not that I'm questioning your wisdom, headmaster, it's that—"

"You're questioning my wisdom." I couldn't

decide whether the owl was annoyed or amused. It was hard to tell with those wide, intense eyes, and feathers covering the entirety of his face and body.

"How will it work, Sir Lancelot?" Nessa asked, her tone one of curiosity.

"I suspect it will be something along the lines of making your house expand within to suit her gigantic size."

"A spell, then?" I asked, working not to take offense at being called "gigantic."

"Magic, surely. But I won't be the one performing it. The school's staff witch Nancy will be more than up for the task, however."

I nodded. What else was I to do? Apparently I was to be squeezed into a house that fit fairies smaller than my hand. That was bound to be … interesting.

Sir Lancelot crossed his wings behind his back and began to pace, probably looking like every headmaster Liana had ever imagined—except for the owl bit, of course. Not even Liana with her flightful imagination had ever anticipated this.

"Until such time as the school singles you out for admission," the owl intoned seriously, "you'll be a guest of the Magical Creatures Academy. With that in mind, you'll behave with the utmost decorum at all times. You'll be respectful and obedient when necessary. But above all"—he paused to smile—"you'll be magical."

Well, the owl didn't seem as fearsome as the fairies had made him out to be. I was almost starting to like him.

"I'll do my best," I said with my own smile.

"I'm sure you will, and that's all that I ask of you. It's the same the Menagerie asks of all its students." Then he nodded succinctly as if he considered the discussion finished.

"Sir, uh, Lancelot?"

"It's my name. No need to tiptoe around it, child."

"Yes, sir. Uh, I mean, what of Quinn?" I paused. "And Irving please."

The owl cocked his head this way and that again while he took me in. "I'm not sure," he finally said, and I was certain it couldn't be a thing he said often. This little headmaster was as self-assured as they made them. "As Quinn is connected to you and the right age for admittance, it's entirely possible that the school will choose him at some point, especially if he's no longer hidden behind his uncle's protections. But that's for Quinn to decide—assuming the school considers him."

"His uncle didn't want him to come here," Fianna said.

"He didn't want Selene to come here either," Nessa added.

"I see," the owl said. "Well, life is rarely what we want it to be or what we think it'll be." He studied me some more. "I'll put feelers out to see what we can find out about the uncle and nephew."

"Oh, thank you," I gushed.

"But I make no guarantee of what we'll be able to do to help them once we find them, assuming they need our help at all."

"I have the feeling they do." The admission pained me.

The owl nodded. "I'll do my best, but my ultimate responsibility is the students and staff of the Menagerie. Even helping you like this is beyond my appointed duties and an extension beyond what I usually offer."

"You're special," Nessa said, just as I'd begun to wonder why the owl was extending his hospitality if he didn't often do it.

"Very special," the diminutive headmaster said. "I know better than most how powerful 'special' can be."

I didn't know what to say to that, particularly when the fairies nodded their agreement, so I didn't say anything as the owl resumed his pacing, wings still clasped behind his back. "Of course, no one wastes their time while they're here, not even the most special ones. You'll train and you'll learn as much as you can about yourself and your magic in preparation for the possibility of admission into the Menagerie."

"I'd love to," I said. "But I need someone to teach me please. I don't know anything about my powers."

"I somehow doubt that."

"I don't, I really don't, I swear." I couldn't understand why I was defending myself by insisting I was an ignoramus.

"We often don't realize what we know until we're forced to prove it."

"She proved that today," Fianna said.

"Indeed," the owl agreed. "But I do believe that there's always something to be learned from a community, hence the institutions of the Magical Creatures Academy and the Magical Arts Academy. I don't plan on leaving you on your own to learn, Lady Selene. Fianna the Crimson and Nessa the Sapphire will help you."

Fianna groaned softly until I threw an accusatory glare her way. *Thanks for the life debt, fairy,* I mentally projected to her. Nessa appeared wary, but at least she didn't complain.

"We're not qualified to teach her," Fianna said. "Our magic is *fae* magic, hers is entirely different."

"And you think I don't realize that?" the owl said with a dangerous lift of his brow. "You'll help her navigate this world that's so unfamiliar to her. Egan will train her." He nodded his head. "Yes, I think that's a very good fit indeed."

The fairies didn't agree or disagree, and I was left wondering who the heck Egan might be.

"Well," the owl said, "I'm needed back at the school. I hope you enjoy your time here, Lady Selene of the Kunu Clan. If I can be of service, don't hesitate to let me know."

Though he suggested he was, I got the feeling he wasn't all that available. Surely running an entire school of supernatural creatures must keep him busy.

To the fairies, he said, "Let me know if you learn anything of the whereabouts of Naomi Nettles or her familiar. We mustn't lose sight of our enemies."

"Of course," Fianna said with a bow of her head. "We'll keep you updated."

"Would you like us to update you on her progress as well?" Nessa asked.

One look from the owl was sufficient response. It said, Of course, this is my school, and I need to know every single thing that transpires involving it. With a final nod and prolonged eye contact with each one of us, he said, "I'll send Egan and Nancy, and I'll send Melinda to help you, Fianna. I do hope your recovery is swift."

"Thank you," Fianna said as the headmaster took off in graceful flight, circled to point back in the direction he came, and disappeared from sight far more quickly than the fairies would have.

I waited what seemed an appropriate time before peppering the fairies with my own questions. "Nancy's a witch?"

"Hm-hm," Nessa said, appearing lost in thought.

"A witch?" I squeaked in alarm.

Fianna chuckled as she moved to straighten out her wings, examining the damage as best she could over her shoulder. "Don't worry, not all witches are like Naomi. As with everything else, there are good witches and bad ones."

"I hope not too many bad ones." My voice was still shrill and I worked to return it to a normal tone.

Fianna grimaced. I already knew I wouldn't like her answer. "There are far too many bad ones—"

"'Dark' ones is the correct term," Nessa said.

"Yes, well, whatever they're called, they're still the worst of news."

"Worse than the creatures after me?" I asked,

breathless. "Worse than the vampire Antonio Dimorelli?"

"Not really. Just as bad, though," Fianna said.

"Oh. I see." I sounded like I was ten years younger. "And, uh, this Egan? Is he a witch too?"

"He'd be a wizard," Nessa said, "if he were a magician. But he's not. He's most definitely not."

"Not a chance," Fianna said.

"Well? What is he, then?"

"He's a centaur. One of the last of his kind," Nessa said.

"A centaur! Aren't they—?"

"Horse men, yes," Fianna said, pretending she was bored.

Nessa chuckled. "He's not just a centaur. He's a pegasus-centaur."

I blinked while I processed. "Then why am I called a sirangel—against my wishes, I might add—and he isn't called a pegataur or something?"

"That's because he won't allow it," Fianna said.

"And none of us is brave enough to try it," Nessa said.

"And no one's scared of me…?"

"Nope." The blue fairy was unapologetic. "When you meet Egan you'll understand."

That's precisely what I was afraid of.

Fianna flew haphazardly to my shoulder and awkwardly patted me. I only realized she was doing it because I turned to look. "It's not as bad as you fear."

"Right," I said, half numb. "And Melinda? Who's she, or what's she, or whatever?"

Nessa smiled fondly. "She's a badger, and the best of folk."

Well, I'd just have to take her word for it, now wouldn't I?

"You'll like her," Nessa continued. "Everyone likes her. She's the mother hen of the school."

"Great," I said, but I didn't have much conviction to put into it.

We sat around for a bit, waiting for Egan, Nancy, and Melinda to arrive I presumed, until Fianna stood from my shoulder and half flitted, half tumbled toward her cousin, who rested on my legs. The warm, bright afternoon sunshine filtered through the tree-tops to sparkle across her broken wings and battered battle outfit, only serving to emphasize her magical nature.

The crimson fairy stared off into the distance in the direction of Sir Lancelot's retreat. "Either they or Sir Lancelot must've gotten caught up in something. We might as well go catch some rest. I know I could use some. My poor wings. I'll need lots of recovery time to heal up."

Nessa offered Fianna a sympathetic grimace. "That's right. You'll heal up and be back to yourself in no time."

"Melinda's pampering will make sure of it," Fianna added. "Let's go." The redheaded fairy cast a forlorn look between her wings and some distant point deeper in the forest.

"Um."

The fairies turned to me.

"Uh, I'm not sure if this is appropriate or not, but, Fianna, would you like me to carry you?"

"Heck yes," she said. "I get enough hard work without making it for myself."

"Me too," Nessa said and eyed the open palm I was extending to her cousin.

"Feel free to join," I told the blue fairy, and she was in my hand before I could finish the sentence.

"Lazy bum," Fianna said, but climbed into my hand next to Nessa. "We're only just over there."

"Where?" I turned, scouring the direction in which she pointed, but I saw no home, none at all.

"That lovely tree stump," Nessa said, pointing too.

"*That* tree stump?"

"The very one." The blue fairy beamed, but I was freaking out.

"There's no way I'll fit in there, no matter what magic this Nancy witch does. It's impossible."

"Don't you worry," Nessa said. "There's not a single truly impossible thing on this entire campus. If fact, we prove the notion wrong on an hourly basis."

I closed the distance between us and the tree stump, shaking my head in disbelief all the while.

"We'll knock the disbelief right out of you in no time," the crimson fairy said, a little too happily.

"Yeah, that's exactly what I'm afraid of."

The fairies laughed and laughed, as if we hadn't just survived a nightmare—and barely. Finally, I couldn't stand to be the only one acting like I'd sucked on a bitter lemon, and I joined in on their laughter. I was either going crazy … or finally joining the world of magic. Only time would determine which of the two it was, and if they weren't one and the same.

As I crossed the glade, my thoughts—and my heart—reached out to Quinn. Wherever he was, I hoped he could feel me. Whatever magical world I was joining, I needed him to share it with me.

I'll find you again, Quinn, I promised. It was a promise I dearly hoped I'd find the way to keep.

"Come on. Hurry up, Selene," Fianna ordered. "I can't wait to be home."

Home. I was so far from the ocean that it seemed I had no choice but to choose a new home.

Nessa giggled. "I don't know how you're going to fit inside, but you'll love it once you do. There's no place more magical than our tree stump."

There certainly would be no place like it, of that I was certain. I moved deeper into the forest to my new home, two fairies nestled in my outstretched palm while the red-haired one pointed the way like a crazed general.

I smiled in relief … or perhaps delirium. I was a guest of the Magical Menagerie. Life could only become more magical.

ANGEL MAGIC

ANGEL MAGIC
Sirangel: Book Two

Continue Selene's adventures in *Angel Magic*!

ACKNOWLEDGMENTS

I'd write no matter what, because telling stories is a passion, but the following people make creating worlds (and life) a joy. I'm eternally grateful for the support of my beloved, James, my mother, Elsa, and my three daughters, Catia, Sonia, and Nadia. They've always believed in me, even before I published a single word. They help me see the magic in the world around me, and more importantly, within.

I'm thankful for every single one of you who've reached out to tell me that one of my stories touched you in one way or another, made you smile or cry, or kept you up long past your bedtime. You've given me reason to keep writing.

ABOUT THE AUTHOR

Lucía Ashta is the Amazon top 100 bestselling author of young adult and new adult paranormal and urban fantasy books, including the series *Magical Creatures Academy*, *Sirangel*, *Magical Arts Academy*, *Witching World*, and *Supernatural Bounty Hunter*.

When Lucía isn't writing, she's reading, painting, or adventuring. Magical fantasy is her favorite, but the action, romance, and quirky characters are what keep her hooked on books.

A former attorney and architect, she's an Argentinian-American author who lives in Sedona with her beloved and three daughters. She published her first story (about an unusual Cockatoo) at the age of eight, and she's been at it ever since.

Sign up for Lucía's newsletter:
https://www.subscribepage.com/LuciaAshta

Connect with her online:
LuciaAshta.com
AuthorLuciaAshta@gmail.com

Hang out with her:
https://www.facebook.com/groups/LuciaAshta/

facebook.com/authorluciaashta

Made in the USA
Middletown, DE
02 April 2021